Jingo

Center Point
Large Print

Also by Max Brand® and available from
Center Point Large Print:

Peyton
The Runaways
Rusty Sabin
The Steel Box
Red Fire
Old Carver Ranch
The Brass Man
Saddlemates
Melody and Cordoba
The Trail Beyond
Mountain Made

Jingo

A Western Story

Max Brand®

CENTER POINT LARGE PRINT
THORNDIKE, MAINE

This Circle Ⓥ Western is published by
Center Point Large Print in 2015 in co-operation with
Golden West Literary Agency.

First Edition, February 2015
Printed in the United States of America
on permanent paper.
Set in 16-point Times New Roman type.

ISBN: 978-1-62899-443-8

Library of Congress Cataloging-in-Publication Data

Brand, Max, 1892–1944.
  Jingo : a western story / Max Brand. — Center Point Large Print
edition.
    pages ; cm
  Summary: "When Jingo decides to court a judge's daughter, he finds
almost everyone out to stop him—the judge, the hopeful suitor, and the
brother of the man he shot over a card game"—Provided by publisher.
  ISBN 978-1-62899-443-8 (hardcover : alk. paper)
  ISBN 978-1-62899-448-3 (pbk. : alk. paper)
  1. Large type books. I. Title.
  PS3511.A87J56 2015
  813′.52—dc23
                                                    2014043963

Chapter One

Jingo: One who believes in a war-like foreign policy. So says the dictionary, but though Jingo's only policy was war-like, and though he treated most people as though they were foreigners, the people who nicknamed him did not have foreign policy in mind.

Conjurers, in the old days, just as they were about to perform a trick, would cry out "Hey, Jingo!" or "Hai, Jingo!" just as at a later date they yelled "Presto!" And out of that expression came the petty oath: By Jingo!

People had some such thing in mind when they called him Jingo, for, in fact, he was a fellow to be either sworn at or sworn by.

He was a thing to fill the eye and warm the heart. He was in his early twenties. He was small enough to lose himself in a crowd, and big enough to punch holes in any member of it. He was as handsome as a wild-caught mustang that has sleeked its sides on the mountain grasses and carries the light of the fire-new morning in its eyes. He was cut out of silk, and he was all from one piece. He feared nothing but the devil, and relied only on his own two strong hands.

This was Jingo as he rode into the town of Tower Creek, under the shadow of Tower

Mountain, filled with a "war-like foreign policy."

He came on an eager mustang with the head of a thoroughbred and an eye that had a jag of red lightning in it. Like horse, like rider.

But though Jingo liked excitement, he found no gratification in fine clothes. His blue flannel shirt was the regular range brand. His sombrero was battered, and the brim of it had been stiffened by passing a rawhide thong through the edge of it. His trousers were as trousers are on the range. He wore a pair of brown leather chaps scarred white by the claws of cactus and mesquite. He had the usual bandanna of red and white around his throat, and only his boots had been made with costly care, and only the long, spoon-handled spurs were things of beauty and of grace. Nevertheless, he always had a way of looking spick-and-span, as though he had been traveling too fast for the dust to catch up and settle on him.

This was Jingo as he rode into Tower Creek. Older men slowed their steps and smiled faintly as they saw him go by. Younger men frowned a little and went on with a thoughtful expression. Mothers doubted him, but their daughters let their hearts come right up in their eyes when they stared at Jingo. For every girl is tempted to throw herself away when she sees a man whose hands may be strong enough to catch her.

It was a big day in Tower Creek. It was the twentieth anniversary of something or other, and

Tower Creek was proud of being twenty years old and still alive to tell about it. There were flags in front of the stores and the saloons. Bunting was strung, fluttering, across the street. And that night there was to be a great dance to which people had come all the way from Blue Water, out of the Blue Water Mountains that looked the color of their name to the north and west, joining the clouds in the sky with the special sheen of snow.

At that particular moment, the best thing that was happening in Tower Creek was a poker game in the back room of Joe Slade's saloon. The most important man in that game was Wally Rankin, gambler and gunman. And the stakes were piling high, particularly in front of Wally, when Jingo, with an instinct truer than that of a homing pigeon, entered that game with his smiling face and his war-like policy.

The sky was the limit. Jingo won $500 in the first ten minutes. At the end of a half hour he was playing in his stocking feet, because he had put up his fine boots and the beautiful spoon-handled spurs that were attached to them. By that time Wally Rankin was smiling faintly, a thing that he rarely allowed himself to do. But, above all things in the world, he loved to "take" a self-confident young fellow. Wally Rankin regarded himself as a moral influence in this world because he was the reef on which it is prophesied by our elders that foolish youth will be wrecked. Wally had wrecked a lot of youths, and he was glad of it, particularly because he always salvaged everything worth taking out of the sinking ship.

Wally was a stern fellow in most of his moods. He looked stern, and he was sterner than his looks. He was six feet three of whalebone and rawhide. His hands were so big that a full-size Colt looked like a boy's water pistol in his grasp, and he could palm half a pack of cards without bending in his thumb. Wally was an honest gambler. That is to say, he never cheated till he had to. Usually the size of his bank roll and the weight of his long experience were sufficient to clean out the heaviest and the luckiest of cowboy gamblers. But if these would not do, Wally knew perfectly well how to take other measures.

Luck, which had dodged Jingo so deftly, now came back and leaned an elbow on his shoulder and laid her cheek against his. He took $1,500 out of that game in the next few minutes, and then held four little sevens over an ace full on a pair of queens that resided in the large grasp of Wally Rankin.

The trouble was that Wally had liked that ace full. It had said something to him in a definite voice. And he pushed out money with free gestures until cold doubt at last laid hands on him and he narrowed his eyes at the handsome, smiling face of Jingo, whose boots were once more on his feet. Wally shoved in $100 to call Jingo's last raise, and then had a chance to see the four little sevens appear on the table—four little sevens like four little brothers, hand in hand. And the three huge aces and the two dignified queens in the possession of Wally Rankin were just big enough to be beaten.

Wally Rankin smiled faintly. He saw that he would have to give the game a new turn, and he did. Inside the outer breast pocket of his coat he had a well-folded, moistened handkerchief, and two sticks of a good dye, one red and one blue. And as he dealt or handled his cards, he began to leave on the backs of them tiny little smudges of blue and red that dried immediately. Presently he could read the backs of those cards as well as he could read their faces. After that the game's fortunes obviously began to favor him. He stopped resting his right hand on the edge of his breast pocket.

That was where he made his mistake. For the eye of Jingo, no matter how bright and careless it was in its rovings, was only a little less acute than that of a hawk in the air or a wolf on the ground. And after a moment or so he began to notice the backs of the cards in his turn.

Finally he said: "Gentlemen, one of us at this table is a dirty, black-hearted, slick-handed, sneaking coyote. The cards have been crooked. The man who did it is carrying a red dye and a blue dye with him. I guess we'd better be searched, all of us."

At the table there was a cattleman who had contributed $2,500 to the game. He could afford the contribution.

Now he stuck out his square jaw and said: "Are you looking at me, young fellow?"

"I'm looking at Mister Rankin," Jingo said, smiling.

Wally Rankin was a very astute fellow, but he mistook the meaning of that smile, and therefore he was a trifle leisurely in his draw. The result was that he showed the gleaming blue steel of his Colt.

But something flashed in the long fingers of Jingo, and Wally was knocked sidelong out of his chair by a bullet that had crashed through his right shoulder.

He was hurt, pained, surprised. But Wally still had a good card up his sleeve. He was just as good with his left hand as he was with his right, and as he lay on the floor, he pulled that second gun. If there had been a stationary target, he would unquestionably had drilled it right through the bull's-eye, because Wally was a man who had long ago learned that he could not afford to miss.

But Jingo was not stationary. At that instant he was, in fact, jumping over the table, and as he landed, he put another bullet into Wally, this time through the left shoulder.

The heart of Wally was strong and determined, but what can a fellow do when he lacks a pair of arms? Wally had to lie still in his blood while

Jingo reached into his breast pocket and produced that telltale pair of dye sticks and the handkerchief that was moistened by the chemical solution.

Well, the town of Tower Creek was a very clannish and patriotic town. It was proud of its leading citizens, of whom Wally Rankin, the "honest" gambler, was one. But there was nothing to be done for him now except to carry him home on a door and mop up the blood on the floor of the saloon.

Jingo lingered long enough to see that the table stakes were divided in equal portions among the other players. Then he went into the bar and gave the bartender $50 to buy drinks all day long "for any tramp that looks thirsty."

He took three fingers of whiskey himself to wet his whistle, for he felt like whistling.

Then Sheriff Vince Cary came in and picked up Jingo and got him into a corner.

The sheriff was a calm man. He looked like the gray of pure iron or fine steel, and that was the stuff that he was made of. He was not young. Many a crook could testify that Vince Cary was too old to be fooled with.

When he had Jingo in a corner, he asked: "Do you know me?"

"Yes," said Jingo. "You're the coroner, aren't you?"

"Coroner?" exclaimed the sheriff. "Why should there be a coroner around here?"

"To look at the body before it's cold," suggested Jingo.

The sheriff made a pause. His brain was strong, but it was not fast. After a time he said: "Young fellow, you don't seem to be a fool. You even seem to know that there may be trouble around this town for you. If that's the case, why don't you ride on while you're able to sit in a saddle?"

"Because," Jingo responded, "I want to see what trouble looks like. I've heard a lot about it. I was beginning to think that it was just one of those things in a book."

The sheriff did not smile. It was a very tough speech, and a very brash speech that he had just heard.

Now he said: "Wally Rankin has a brother, as I suppose you've heard."

"I haven't heard," said Jingo, "but he looked like a fellow who might have something good at home."

"Jake Rankin is good," said the sheriff. "He's so good that he's never been taken."

"He's trouble, is he?" Jingo asked.

"That's his first name. As soon as he gets a chance to find you alone . . ."

"It's hard to be alone in this town," Jingo said, "but I'll try."

"What do you think of this town?" asked the sheriff.

"Why, it's a nice little place," Jingo answered.

"Nice and quiet. A good place for an invalid. The sort of a place where a man could rest. A lot of lungers would like to find a place like this to die in. It's the sort of air that has bubbles in it, and a lot of sparkle. A good town for old men to get older in, I should say."

The sheriff considered this glibness, and again he failed to smile.

"Young man," he said, "this town has a large cemetery. The cemetery is quite a feature of this here town."

"I thought so," said Jingo. "Even mountain air can't cure every disease."

"A lot of people have enjoyed a sudden death around here," went on the sheriff. "Matter of fact, there seems to be something dangerous in the air. I dunno what. But I could tell a man the minute I see his face whether the air of this town would be dangerous or not. It's a kind of a gift that I've got. The minute I seen your face I knew that you'd better move on."

"Thanks," said Jingo. "But the fact is that I've got to stay on here. I've got to meet somebody."

"Who?"

"I don't know," said Jingo. "I've just got a feeling that I've got to meet somebody here."

The sheriff started scowling. He was very angry. For one thing, he loved his town, and it angered him to the very heart to hear a young adventurer make light of it.

"Who are you?" he asked.

"You mean, who are my folks, and everything like that?"

"That's what I mean," the sheriff said.

"My father is old Joseph Isaac Jingo," said Jingo. "Maybe you've heard of him."

"I haven't," said the sheriff. "What did you say the last name was?"

"He's a very respected citizen," Jingo continued. "Joseph Isaac Jingo is his name."

The sheriff stared into the grave face of Jingo.

"The devil that's his name," he said in disbelief.

"The devil it isn't," said Jingo.

"Young feller, are you trying to pull my leg?"

"Your leg seems to be long enough already," said Jingo. "Joseph Isaac Jingo is my father's name. Some people call him Jig for short."

"Yeah, I'll bet they do," said the sheriff. "Did he ever dance on air, eh?"

Jingo smiled gently.

"What part of the country d'you come from, anyway?" asked the sheriff.

"Well," Jingo said, "I wish you could see the place. A beautiful corner of the world, Sheriff . . . you *are* a sheriff, aren't you?"

"Yes. I'm the sheriff."

"I thought so," Jingo said. "I can always tell a sheriff by a certain tired look around the mouth and a lost look about the eyes. But, speaking of the part of the country I come from . . . ah, there's a place to see, Sheriff. There's a section where the cattle *are* cattle. There's a place where the longhorns grow bigger and fatter than shorthorns any place else. I wish I could tell you, Sheriff, about the way the hills roll back to the mountains, and the berry thickets along the creeks, and the big trees in the uplands, and the deer that any boy can pot with a Twenty-Two, and the trout in the streams like bits of sunshine flashing, and the old white buildings on the ranches, and the farm lands in the river bottoms, and the cattle everywhere, big, bright-colored pools of 'em gathered close together under the shadows of the trees in the heat of the day."

"That sounds like a country to me," mused the sheriff dreamily. "Good country for sheep?"

"It's a strange thing," said Jingo, "but sheep-herders never seem to have any luck in that part of the world. A lot of times they've started to drive in their flocks for the open range, but something always happens. The sheep get along very well. They like the grass. They start to get fat, but there's something about the air that dries up the sheepherders and makes them disappear. And when the shepherds are gone, you know that a flock won't last long. The wolves come and get the sheep."

The sheriff laughed heartily.

"That sounds good to me. That sounds like a real

man's country," said Sheriff Cary. "Got a town around there?"

"A town? The best town you ever saw," said Jingo. "There's a church in the middle of it, and a pair of swimming pools on the edge of it, a school for the boys to play hooky from, and plenty of lights for the cowpunchers to shoot out on Saturday night."

The sheriff laughed again. "What did you say the name of that town was?" he asked.

"Jingoville," Jingo answered without smiling.

The sheriff started violently out of his pleasant daydream.

"Are you kidding me?"

"Kidding you?" Jingo repeated seriously. "Kidding you? Kidding a *sheriff?* No, no, sir. I wouldn't do that. I want you to understand that I was raised to respect sheriffs. I was properly raised, and taught to be respectful to old women, and half-wits, and sheriffs."

Sheriff Cary raised his hand and tugged down his sombrero a little over his eyes so that they were lost in a deeper shadow. He stared for a moment.

"You must be tired standing," Jingo said. "Take this chair. I'll order you a drink, if I may. A nice, cold milk shake with a dash of sherry to flavor it would be about the thing, I should say."

The sheriff turned on his heel and left the saloon.

Chapter Two

Enough of this conversation had been heard for all the bystanders to know what had gone on. And since there were very few people in Tower Creek who dared to badger the sheriff, and since everyone always wishes to take a fall out of the powers of the law, there was a good, hearty laugh from the crowd in the barroom as the sheriff went outside. The saloonkeeper, Joe Slade, rubbed his knuckles across his thick, loose lips and laughed the loudest of the lot.

"I hear you say that you came from Jingoville?" he asked.

"That's right," said Jingo. "You know the place?"

"I've got a second cousin of my sister's aunt living there right now," said the bartender. "He stays there for his complexion and the shooting."

Jingo rested his foot on the bar and called for another drink.

"When the season comes in," he said, "all you can hear, from morning to night, is the booming of the guns in the hills, as steady as the roaring of waterfalls in the spring floods. That's the way it is when the season opens in Jingoville."

"The season for shooting what?" asked a bystander.

"Grasshoppers," Jingo stated, and pushed back from the bar.

He left the saloon while the uproar was still continuing, and went out onto the street.

"Where is Jake Rankin?" he asked a man at the first corner.

The man had a sour face and a sour temper.

"Jake Rankin lives at the corner of Hope Alley and Hell Street," he said, and walked on down the boardwalk.

Jingo was pleased. He liked what he had heard, and he liked the set of the stranger's shoulders, and the towering height of him. He hurried to catch up with him.

"Tell me about yourself, brother," said Jingo. "It seems that I've met you somewhere. In a dream, perhaps."

"I meet a lot of people . . . in crowds," said the big man.

"It's your eyes and your smile, I guess," said Jingo. "They've been haunting me."

The big man halted, put his hand on a hitch rack, and stared.

"All that I can't remember is your name," said Jingo.

"I haven't got a name," said the stranger.

"Your parents never able to make up their minds?" Jingo commented with sympathy.

"No. Up in my part of the country they never give names to the kids. They just say 'You.'"

"You're just a sort of a roustabout up there?" asked Jingo.

"That's all. I help out in the kitchen, too, and dry the dishes after dinner, and get the mail, and run the errands. What's your name, mister?"

"Jingo is my name."

"That's a good name. Jingle is a good name for a gent that rattles such a lot. Your folks have got you all dressed up in long pants, I see."

"I dress up like a man once a week," said Jingo. "It'd surprise you what a lot of people I fool."

"I'll bet it would," said the big fellow. "If you're through remembering about me, I'll go along."

"I'm sorry you're not going my way," Jingo said. "I thought maybe you were a neighbor of Jake Rankin on Hell Street."

"Are you going to see Jake on that street?"

"I hear he intends looking me up, so I thought I'd just call on him and save his time."

"What you intend to peddle on Hell Street?" asked the big man.

"Lead," Jingo answered.

"That's heavy stuff for a kid in his first pair of long pants."

"It's easy to sell, though," said Jingo.

"Yeah, if you can make the right kind of a talk. Maybe I'll walk along with you, after all. We'll go this way."

19

He turned and went up the street with Jingo.

"What part of the world d'you come from?" the stranger asked.

"Jingoville," said Jingo. "Maybe you've heard about that town?"

"Where the pastures is all covered with blue forget-me-nots? Is that the place?"

"That's the place. They graze herds of suckers."

"There's always a market for that sort of meat," said the big man.

His sour, long, heavy-featured face relaxed in something that approximated a smile.

"Still," Jingo said, "I can't place the right name for you."

"Some people call me the Parson. But I never studied for the church, neither."

"It all comes back to me," said Jingo. "Of course, you're the Parson."

"And how long might you've known Jake Rankin?" asked the Parson.

"I never met him," said Jingo. "But I met his brother a little while back."

"You know Wally? He ain't lucky, I'd say. He's kind of a mongrel."

"What's the cross?" asked Jingo.

"Fast brains and slow hands. They never come to no good," said the Parson.

"I hope," said Jingo, "that Jake Rankin is a purebred one, though."

"He's all right," answered the Parson. "If you don't believe me, go and knock at the door of that house and ask for Jake. He only stands about five two, but he can win a lot of races with two guns up in the saddle."

Chapter Three

Jingo saw a little unpainted shack that had for a front yard a hitch rack with plenty of hoof holes pawed into the bare dirt. Boards from apple boxes had been nailed up to take the place of several missing panes in the windows, and the stovepipe leaned awry above the roof.

"Nobody's wasted any time keeping up the face of that house," Jingo commented.

"It ain't the stable that counts, but the horse inside it," said the Parson.

"So long," said Jingo.

"I'll wait here. If you get throwed, I might haul you to a piece of soft ground to lie on," answered the Parson.

So Jingo crossed the street, singing softly to himself. As he came toward the front door of the shack, he heard groans distinctly that welled heavily through the interior of the little house. He knocked at the door.

"Who the devil?" asked a harsh voice.

"Flowers for Wally," Jingo said.

A rapid footfall approached the front door. It was jerked open, and Jingo found himself looking at a small edition of Wally Rankin. A smaller edition and a harder one. The iron of Wally had been hammered down to the rigid, compacted steel of a smaller frame. The stern mind of Wally had been concentrated to a burning point that glinted out of the eyes of his older brother.

"What kind of funny business you got in your head, drunk?" Jake Rankin asked. "And who are you, anyway?"

"My name is Jingo," he answered, and smiled.

Jake Rankin grew calm.

"So you're the gent, are you?" he said.

"Thank you," said Jingo. "I heard that you might be looking for me. So I thought I'd save your shoe leather."

"Who told you that I'd be looking for you?" asked Jake.

"The sheriff."

"The sheriff's a thoughtful sort of an *hombre*," Jake Rankin remarked. "One of these days he's going to think himself right into a grave of some kind or other. Listen to me, kid."

"Yes, sir," said Jingo.

"And none of your lip," Jake said.

"No, sir," said Jingo.

Jake Rankin licked his lips and ran his hungry eyes over the lithe body of Jingo. He was a judge of men, was Jake, and he could appreciate the way the parts of Jingo were fitted together. He handled him with his eyes the way a horse dealer handles a horse, judging bone and sinew, and the quality of the long muscles that make for speed, or the bulging muscles that make lifting strength.

The muscles of Jingo were all long and cunningly worked together. He looked as capable of speed, say, as a well-braided whiplash of new leather.

Jake Rankin missed not a single point.

"Jingo," he said, "it ain't hard to see that you been well raised, and you know when to go and pay your respects to your elders. Now I'm going to explain something to you. Walk down the hall and look into the back room without letting yourself be seen, will you?"

Jingo hesitated as long as a running horse pauses at a jump.

"Sure," he said, and walked right in through the open door and past the grim face of Jake Rankin, so that his back was presently turned on that famous warrior.

Down the hallway, with a very careful, soundless step moved Jingo, pausing at the door of the back room. That door was half ajar, and through the crack at the back of it he could see a widening slice of the room. He could see the head and the heavily bandaged shoulders of Wally Rankin, and he could see an old, gray-headed woman sitting by the bed, her shoulders hunched up as she leaned toward the invalid. The head of Wally kept turning uneasily from side to side as the agony burned him deeper and deeper.

Then a great groan came shuddering out of his throat again.

The old woman said: "Shame on you, Wally. Shame on a man actin' like a dog that's been run over. Shame on the throat that'll go mournin' for pain, like a lovesick wolf. Shame on a man that'll bray like a fool of a donkey in the middle of the night. I wouldn't own you. I wouldn't have you if I thought you didn't have nothin' better inside of you."

Wally was silent.

The agony struck him again with a heavy hand, but though his lips furled back over the glistening white of his teeth, he uttered not a sound. The bright sweat ran down his face as he endured in silence.

Jingo came slowly back down the hallway and confronted Jake Rankin.

"Thanks, Jake," he said. "I understand."

He stepped outside the doorway and paused a moment politely.

"I'll have to be going along," he said.

"Wait a minute and have a drink with me," suggested Jake.

"Any liquor you gave me would suit me fine," Jingo answered. "But I've got a friend waiting for me across the street."

"Ask him in, too," Jake Rankin suggested. "I ain't seen the Parson for a long spell." And Jake stepped out and waved.

The Parson, with enormous, slow strides, crossed the street and came up to them.

"We're having a drink, Parson," said Jake. "Come along in and join us."

There was no handshaking between the pair.

The Parson said: "Sure. I guess your whiskey ain't spoiled."

The three of them went into the front room. It was the ghost of a parlor. There was a faded round rug on the floor, and a round center table on the middle of the rug, with a brass-bound Bible, *Robinson Crusoe*, and a picture album on it. Some striped wallpaper was beginning to come off the wall in tatters.

Jake Rankin disappeared and came back again, carrying three heavy glasses and a stone jug. He tilted the weight of the jug with one hand, over his forearm, and poured out three large drinks of the whiskey.

"It's thirty years old, and it's lost all its teeth," Jake advised.

"There was never anything cheap about a Rankin," said the Parson thoughtfully. "That was a good doctor you sent me, Jake."

"Yeah, he was good," Jake agreed. "He fixed you up pretty good, I see."

"I limp a little in cold weather," said the Parson. "Otherwise, you wouldn't know nothing. A funny thing how clean your bullets went through me."

"They seemed to kind of dodge the bones, I guess," Jake surmised. "Maybe I'll have better luck next time."

"Yeah," said the Parson. "I'm getting ready for the next time."

"I'm always ready," said Jake. "Which I mean I gotta kind of apologize to the kid here."

"Don't mention it," Jingo said.

"I mean," Jake Rankin went on, "him walking all the way here on his feet and tiring himself out and getting all dusty to give me a fair chance at him. But the old woman has had kind of a shock, seeing Wally brought home on a door today. She's kind of partial to Wally, even if he's a bum with a gun. She kind of likes him. He's the baby of the family, if you know what I mean."

"Sure," said the Parson.

"It might put her back a lot," Jake said, "if she was to hear of a second gunfight in the family in one day. It might be kind of rough on her."

He set his jaws at the end of this speech. The muscles stood out in great ridges. The fore part of his face seemed to sharpen; his eyes narrowed. He looked like a wolf about to leap into a fight.

Only then was Jingo able to appreciate the frightful effort of self-control that Jake Rankin was using.

"You take a woman," said the Parson, "and hitting them twice in the same place is what breaks them up. You gotta be careful."

"That's what I thought about Ma," Jake Rankin said. "Just the same, I'm mighty sorry to disappoint you, Jingo. You coming up here to see me was mighty handsome, is all I gotta say."

"Don't mention it," Jingo said. "We'll meet again. How's Wally coming along?"

"He'll never use his left hand again," Jake answered.

"That's too bad," remarked Jingo. "Because he was twice as fast with his left hand as he was with his right."

"You got the eye to see with," remarked Jake, nodding. "He was straighter with his left, too. Well, here's to you, boy. Here's to you, Parson. I hope I get a chance to put some lead through you before long."

"All right," said the Parson. "Here's hoping that we meet head-on along a one-way trail. And heaven help the one that's gotta go over the edge."

"Here's to you, Jingo," went on Jake Rankin. "I dunno when a young gent has pleased me much more'n you pleased me today. Walking down the hall with your back to me . . . that was pretty good. Believe me, I'm going to really enjoy cutting the heart out of you, Jingo."

"Thanks," Jingo said, holding up his glass. "Here's in your eye, Jake. The next thing you get from me will be a lot heavier than good wishes."

They tilted their glasses at their lips, and Jingo, after tasting the excellent old whiskey, let it roll very slowly down his throat. He put down the glass with a sigh of pleasure.

"That," he said, "is the pure quill."

"Have another, Jingo," urged Jake Rankin.

"I'd like to," Jingo said. "But I've had one drink today already. And more than two is more than my rule. What with all the sport that a fellow can find if he looks around in this town."

Jake Rankin smiled.

He accompanied the two through the front door and stood there, resting his elbow on the hitch rack.

"Glad to've seen you boys," said Jake.

"You'll be seeing us again," said the Parson.

"But one at a time," added Jingo.

Jake held up a hand in protest.

"I know a gentleman when I see one," he said seriously. "It's going to be a pleasure. It's going to be a real pleasure. I'm going to look forward to it. Shall I give your regards to Wally, Jingo?"

"Give him my best regards," Jingo said. "I'll try to find something he likes and send it to him. Does he take to venison?"

"Venison is his favorite fruit."

"I'll have a deer here by night," said Jingo, "if I have to go out and get it myself. So long, Jake."

"So long, Jingo."

So Jingo walked back downtown with the Parson, and they said not a word to one another all the way. Speech was not needed between them just then.

Chapter Four

As they went down the street through the warmth of the late afternoon, Jingo said: "Parson, it sort of appeared to me that you were a little off your feed when I first met you. Or does your face always look like that when you haven't got a feedbag tied to it?"

"Jingo," the Parson said, slowing his step a little, "it kind of comes over me that I gotta do something about you one of these days, and maybe this is the day."

"You don't follow my drift," Jingo said. "The fact is I'm making friendly motions."

"You are?" the Parson said skeptically. "Because if you ain't . . ."

"I am," Jingo assured, "and I don't want any part of the bad time that you could give a man."

At this the Parson relented.

"You son of a double-jointed lightning flash," he murmured, "it sure does me good to hear you talk soft. Which I wouldn't mind saying that I was a trifle peeved some time ago, and I'm still peeved. And I wouldn't mind telling you the reason, neither . . . which is I've gone and lost Lizzie."

"You've lost her?" Jingo said, regarding with a side glance the long and frightfully ugly face of his new friend.

"I've lost Lizzie," the Parson repeated, shaking his head sadly.

"How?"

"I got drunk," said the Parson. "I got boileder than an owl, and I lost Lizzie."

"Sometimes they act up when a fellow puts on the paint," agreed Jingo. "How boiled did you get?"

"Faro, and a lot of noise."

"Cleaned out?"

"Clean as a whistle."

"Tell me about Lizzie, will you?" asked Jingo.

"That's a thing that I don't like to talk about much. It kind of gripes me when I think about losing Lizzie."

"What's she like, though?"

"There ain't anything like her. She's all by herself."

"Pretty?"

"To me she's beautiful," said the Parson. "There's some that differ. There's some that say she's too big in the head and too lean in the neck. There's some that say her legs ain't all that they should be. She's kind of humped in the back, too. But to me she's beautiful. Lizzie is the kind," the Parson said, looking into the distance in the pale sky, "Lizzie is the kind that will stay with you. She'll never let you down, and she'll never say no."

"The kind you can depend upon, eh?" Jingo said sympathetically.

"Exactly. Day or night, Lizzie is ready for the fun. She's ready to step out and travel."

"Just for you, or for any of the boys?"

"For any of the boys?" exclaimed the Parson. "What would I be mourning about if Lizzie was one that anybody could take in hand? No, sir. I'm the only man in the world that can handle her. And I'm the only man in the world that puts the full worth on her. It's going to practically break her heart when she finds that I'm gone for good. And she's going to maybe never forgive me for selling her out."

"Hold on," protested Jingo soberly. "You sold her out?"

"I sold her out and let her go. I was drunk," the Parson affirmed sadly.

"That's bad," murmured Jingo, frowning at the ground. And he drew away from his companion.

"The night"—the Parson paused to sigh—"was the time when Lizzie sort of shone. You couldn't see her so good by night, and she sort of shone. She got a second wind, and she could go all night till the morning. I never seen anything like it. We've traveled some long hikes together."

"She's traveled with you a lot, has she?" Jingo asked, with a growing distaste showing in his face.

"Her? Traveled a lot with me?" The Parson laughed scornfully. "Nobody ever traveled any farther with a man than Lizzie traveled with me.

We've gone tramping a hundred and twenty miles between water holes in the desert, the two of us have. Is that traveling?"

"Great thunder," Jingo said. "Yes, that's traveling. It's hard to believe."

"That's what other folks say. But I know. I measured them miles by the hours we staggered along together. Them hours was days long. But we pulled through to water together."

He added, after a moment: "And now she's gone. Maybe I'll never see her again. There's a one-eyed hound of a Mex half-breed that had his eye on her, and he'll get her, sure."

"Great thunder," Jingo said again. "Something has to be done."

"There ain't nothing can be done," declared the Parson.

"But will she go with the greaser?" Jingo asked.

"How can she help it? I sold her out, didn't I?"

"I don't understand," Jingo said. "My brain is sort of whirling a little. But . . . maybe she'll get used to the new life, eh?"

He looked on his companion with a nameless disgust as he spoke.

"She's too old," the Parson declared huskily.

Through his teeth Jingo said: "Well, how old is she?"

"Twelve years," answered the Parson.

"Twelve years!" Jingo gasped.

"And fit as a fiddle. A little bit over at the knees, maybe, but nothing to speak of. I like 'em over at the knees a little, don't you? It kind of eases their gait a little."

"You mean to say that a twelve-year-old girl . . . ?" Jingo cried.

"Girl? You fool! I mean a mare," broke in the Parson.

Jingo leaned against a wall and laughed and groaned and laughed again.

"I thought Lizzie was your girl," he said. "I was getting ready to slam you for a hound, Parson."

"I wish that she was only a girl," the Parson said. "There's plenty more of females in the world, but there's only one Lizzie."

"What did you get for her?"

"Only a hundred and fifty. I was drunk." The Parson let out another sigh.

"What did you pay for her?"

"Two hundred in hard cash, and five years of constant fighting," answered the Parson. "There was times when I thought that Lizzie had me licked. But finally I won out. She's a tough mare, Jingo."

"Where is she now?"

"Down at Morgan's, the horse dealer's. Why?"

"We'll go down there and look at her," Jingo announced.

"I wouldn't want to," remarked the Parson. "It would just kind of wring me, if you follow that. It would just sort of stir me all up, and I wouldn't settle down for a couple of days, maybe."

"Well," said Jingo, "I'll buy her back for you."

"You'll which?"

"I'll buy her back," Jingo said. "Come on to Morgan's with me."

The Parson was too deeply moved for words. He was so deeply moved that he silently took from his rear pocket a great cut of plug tobacco, well compressed and hardened by time. Through a corner of the plug his powerful teeth sheared with a snap. He offered the plug to Jingo, who shook his head. The Parson shook his in turn, but for another reason. He walked on with Jingo, still silently.

They reached Morgan's.

There was a long shed, a shack with living quarters at one end of it, and a tangle of corral fences, with a continual swirl of dust going up like smoke into the air. Morgan himself was a withered little man, with only two prominent features—his nose and his Adam's apple.

The Parson paid little attention to the little horse dealer. Instead, he went to the fence and leaned his huge, gaunt elbows on it.

"There's Lizzie," he said softly to Jingo.

"Which one?" asked Jingo.

"Which one?" snapped the Parson. "There ain't more than one in that corral to anybody with an eye for horseflesh."

Jingo followed the direction of the Parson's glance.

"You mean that brindle plow horse over there?" Jingo asked. "The one with a head like a moose and a neck like a blue crane?"

The Parson said nothing. He did not so much as turn his head. But his great shoulders gradually hunched up toward his ears, and his ears turned red, and his enormous hands slowly contracted into fists.

Jingo said: "Well, that brindle roan, or whatever you call the color, has some points, after all. She's all points, in a manner of speaking. Withers and knees and, hocks and ribs, and the top of her head and her chin . . . and her hips sticking out like a pair of sharp elbows under a kimono . . . Matter of fact, I never saw a horse with so many points."

The huge body of the Parson began to straighten. He reached back slowly, took a firm grip on the belt of Jingo and the back of his trousers, and, with that one mighty hand, hoisted him up so that his feet came to rest on the second bar of the fence.

"Now you're up where you can look better," said the Parson. "How does she look to you now?"

"Now that I look again," Jingo said, squirming a little because the hand of the Parson was gripping a good deal more than cloth and leather, "now that I look again, I'd say that Lizzie is one of the most extraordinary horses that I ever saw."

"There is things about your vocabulary, son," said the Parson, "that had oughta be straightened out, and maybe one of these here days I'll take time off and do the straightening."

Suddenly he relaxed his hold and sighed.

"Look," said the Parson. "She sees me, and she knows me. Dog-gone her heart, look at that. She knows me, Jingo."

Lizzie had suddenly twitched back her long, mulish ears. She stared straight at her old master with red danger in her eyes.

"Yeah, it seems as though she knows you," Jingo said, grinning. "She certainly knows you."

"She could pick me right out of a crowd," the Parson said, and sighed. "See that? She knows me, all right. Good old girl."

Lizzie had actually turned about, and, looking back with a twist of her head, she lifted a tentative hind hoof, as though prepared to kick.

"She knows me," mourned the Parson. "No matter what happens, nobody else is ever going to mean to Lizzie what I meant to her."

"Morgan," broke in Jingo as the horse dealer came near them, "what's the price on that brindle roan over there? I need a plow horse for slow work."

Morgan smiled faintly.

"Two hundred and fifty," he said after some contemplating.

"Cents?" Jingo said. "Well, I'll take her, then, if

you'll throw in a saddle and a bridle and a lead rope."

"Two hundred and fifty or three hundred *dollars*," Morgan corrected Jingo. "I dunno that I'd let her go at that, except that I need the coin just now."

"I thought you'd pay somebody to lead her out of the corral," Jingo said as he climbed down from the fence. "What's she good for?"

"She's good," Morgan said, "for carrying two hundred and thirty pounds a hundred miles in a day."

"What?" Jingo cried. "She doesn't look as though she could get herself into a lope."

"She can't, but she can trot," Morgan said. "And she can trot all day. I've tried her, and I know. She kind of mixes up a gent's floating ribs with his inmost wishes, but she never stops going."

"Morgan," broke out the Parson, "as long as I had to sell her, I'm glad that I sold her to a gent with brains."

"I'll give you two hundred flat for her," Jingo said. "Here's the money."

"Two hundred and fifty, and I'm robbing myself, at that," insisted Morgan.

"She's not worth bargaining," answered Jingo. "Here's the rest of the cash. Fellows like you, Morgan, are what keep young men out of business. They take to bank robbing instead, because they see that it's all the same idea, except that bank robbing doesn't hurt the feelings of the banker so much. Lead out that chunk of a wooden horse, will you? And we'll see if she can move."

Lizzie was led forth, therefore. The saddle and bridle that had been stripped off her were replaced, and Jingo said to the Parson: "There's your beautiful Lizzie. Take her, Parson. And I hope faro never puts you asunder again."

"You mean I'm to take her like that?" said the Parson.

He jerked his hat down over his eyes and approached Lizzie. It was not an easy thing to do. At the sight of her old master, she made a desperate effort to buck off her saddle, squealing like a hurt pig.

The Parson paused and remarked: "She's got spirit, Jingo. You can see that for yourself. A whole lot of spirit. And if . . . ."

He broke off his speech to seize an interval of comparative quiet in the evolutions of Lizzie, and, running in, he flung himself into the saddle.

Lizzie, at the same time, pointed her nose at the sky and followed it as far as her long legs would hurl her into the air. She landed on springs, apparently, and for five full minutes she fought like a great raw-boned tiger. Suddenly she was still, and stood with her head down and her long ears flattened against her neck.

"She knows me again," the Parson announced

proudly. "There ain't anybody in the world that she acts up for like that."

"Anybody else would be dead," Jingo observed. "Come on along with me and we'll feed our faces."

They went down the street to a restaurant, where the Parson declared that he was capable of eating a light lunch. Jingo dined heartily enough, but when he had finished, the long procession of steaks, fried eggs, potatoes in heaps, sections of white loaf smeared thick with butter, and then wedge after monstrous wedge of apple pie, continued to drift down the throat of the Parson, borne along on a river of steaming black coffee.

When he had finished, he rolled a cigarette and burned up half of it with one vast inhalation. After that single breath, smoke spouted from his mouth and nose for a full minute as he made a speech.

He said: "Jingo, you got faults. You ain't got an eye for a good horse when you see one, and you're fresh. You're mighty fresh. But horses you can be taught about, and you can study Lizzie every day, and I can salt you down a bit, too, from time to time. Besides all this, you got a few good points, and I reckon that I could get along with you. I reckon that maybe I'll go to work for you."

"I haven't got enough for you to work on," said Jingo. "I don't own a ranch, if that's what you mean."

"I never said you did," the Parson said. "But you own a lot of spare time. I'll go to work on that."

"What would you do with it?" Jingo asked.

"I'd build fence and ride range on your spare time," said the Parson. "I'd keep trouble away from it and the whole range free and easy. When you fall on your nose, I'll pick you up, and every time you're kicked out the door of a saloon, I'll be standing in the street, ready to catch you and ease the drop."

Jingo grinned.

"What pay would you want for that sort of work?" he asked finally.

"Three dollars a day . . . and board," said the Parson.

"Suppose I pay you ten dollars a day and you board yourself," Jingo suggested, looking at the great heaps of emptied dishes.

"No," the Parson said, grinning in turn, "I wouldn't want to put myself on a diet."

"Maybe you know," said Jingo, "that any rancher around here can get all the cowpunchers he wants . . . experienced hands . . . at forty dollars a month?"

"Sure, I know it," answered the Parson. "But what one of 'em would take the job rounding up the spare time of Jingo?"

"Well," Jingo said, "I'm going to hire you out of curiosity. Here's your first job. There's a dance in this town tonight. All day I've been seeing Tower

Creek, and it's only fair that Tower Creek should have a chance to see me. Find out about that dance. Get the name of the prettiest girl in town. Then come back to the hotel. I'll be there in my room, sleeping a couple of hours. So long, Parson."

Chapter Five

Jingo was very tired. He had not closed his eyes for thirty-six hours. Therefore, when he reached the hotel, he picked out a room, locked the door once inside, shoved two Colts under the pillow, and then fell face down on the bed and went to sleep.

When a knock came at the door, he dragged himself to it, turned the key in the lock, and saw the towering bulk of the Parson standing before him. Then he staggered back to the bed, fell once more on his face, and was instantly and profoundly asleep.

It was twilight. Therefore the Parson lit the lamp, trimmed the wick, settled the chimney down, and went to look at his new friend and employer. He slid his hands under the pillow, found the two guns, and laid them on the table, smiling a little. Then he went to the water pitcher, dipped a towel into it, and, returning to the bed, he jerked the sleeper over on his back and dropped the sopping towel in his face.

The towel hit the opposite wall as Jingo landed on his feet in the middle of the room. The monstrous form of the Parson was leaning beside the window, his long, sour face distorted by a twisting smile.

"I've got a mind," said Jingo, "to paste you on the nose."

"Don't you do it," said the giant. "You whang me on the chin or slam me in the stomach, and I won't mind it none. You'll get plenty of exercise, and my feelings won't be hurt. But this here nose of mine is kind of delicate, ever since Lizzie kicked it sideways, one day. It was the first day that I ever met Lizzie, and dog-gone me if she ain't been in my thoughts ever since. Leave my nose alone, son, or I might get all excited."

"I've got a good idea," said Jingo, "that I can lick you, or two like you, Parson."

"It's an idea, but it ain't any good," said the Parson. "I'll tell you why it ain't any good. Nobody licks me, without a gun. If we was out on a thousand-acre lot, maybe you'd play tag with me a while and get away with it, but these here four walls are too dog-gone' close together. You wouldn't have no room to think in here, Jingo."

Jingo got a second towel and dried his face. He sat on the edge of the table and smoked a cigarette.

"Maybe you're right," he observed, "but one of these days we'll have to have it out. I couldn't stay friends with a man I didn't fight."

"Sure you couldn't," answered the Parson. "I can understand that. I feel the same way, and that's why I ain't got any friends. When I get through fighting a gent, he has to go to a hospital and stay there so long that he forgets what happened to him in the first place. All that I remind him of afterward is doctor bills."

"Sit down," said Jingo. "And tell me about the dance."

"The dance," said the Parson, "is going to be a humdinger. They got an orchestra with two slide trombones in it. I heard one of them slide trombones practicing, and it sounded like Lizzie snoring. It made me feel dog-gone' homesick."

"Who goes to the dance?" asked Jingo.

"The whole of Tower Creek," answered the giant.

"And who's the best girl in the town?" asked Jingo.

"The best girl in the town comes from out of the town," said the Parson. "Clean all the way down from Blue Water."

"She's come a long way to meet me," said Jingo, "but I'll make it worth her while."

The Parson shook his vast head and made a cigarette with care, the wisp of paper turning slowly in his enormous fingertips.

"She ain't for you, boy," he declared. "She's a special preserve."

"It's the kind I like," said Jingo.

"She ain't for you," the Parson repeated. "She's got some slick Easterners along with her, and they're going to fill up her whole landscape."

"I've been East myself," Jingo said.

"So have I," said the Parson. "I been all the way East to Denver, but you and me never been as East as she's been . . . her and her young men."

"I've got an idea that she's going to like me a whole lot," Jingo assured the Parson.

"You wouldn't have the right idea at all," said the Parson. "She's nice."

"So am I," Jingo said. "I can be so nice you never saw anything like it. Have you seen her?"

"I seen her go down the street," said the Parson. "She's got a nice brown face and a nice pair of blue eyes, and her clothes is made so that you know where she is inside them."

"What is her moniker?" asked Jingo.

"By name of Tyrrel," answered the Parson. "She's old Judge Tyrrel's gal, is what she is."

"Tyrrel?" Jingo said. "I think I've heard the name somewhere."

"Well, maybe you have, at that," remarked the Parson. "You might've seen it on twenty or thirty buildings in some of the big towns. Or you might've seen it over some oil wells. Or maybe it was chalked up over any one of half a dozen gold mines. And half the cows in Texas bawl 'Tyrrel' when they're on the road."

"No, I think I found the name in a book," said Jingo.

"Yeah. And there's been books wrote about him, too. He's one of these here empire builders, if you know what I mean. He's a Maker of the West, and a Big Man, and one of the Most Remarkable Men in the Country. He lays cornerstones with a gold trowel and he's the head of the committee of big birds that gives the bouquet of cactus to the visiting Queen of Egypt. He calls the President by his nickname, and the train makes a special stop for folks that want to get off and see the front face of Judge Tyrrel's house."

"I must have met him somewhere," said Jingo, "and it's a cinch that I'm going to meet his daughter in Tower Creek."

"What makes you feel so good?" asked the Parson.

"I don't feel so good," Jingo said. "No honest, earnest worker feels very good when he thinks about retiring. But it seems to me that I'd better retire to the Tyrrel millions, brother."

"You take an imagination like you got," commented the Parson, "and you waste yourself, son. You oughta write books and things. What's the hard and honest work that you been doing all your long life?"

"Ah, Parson," said Jingo, "time is not alone what counts. The number of the years may be short, but responsibility is what ages us, young or old. Many a man, Parson, is still young-hearted at seventy . . . and many a man of twenty-five is already bowing his head toward the earth."

"That's great," said the Parson. "You could put the boys to sleep in church just as good as if you was a salaried minister and was paid for the work."

"A trifle, a trifle," said Jingo. "You've never heard my line really working, Parson. When I start, the guinea hens stop sounding off in the barnyard, and the wild geese come down out of the sky to listen. You've never really heard me honk."

The Parson looked at him with an indulgent eye. "What I mean," he said, "is this. If you try to crowd that Tyrrel girl tonight, there's going to be trouble popping. Understand?"

"It sort of saddens me, Parson," answered Jingo. "What grieves me is that a fellow like you, with a head your size, shouldn't have more brains behind the eyes. I've told you that I'm going to give the girl a dizzy rush tonight. I've told you that I intend to retire on the Tyrrel millions, if I can stand the girl's face. And still you don't seem to believe me."

The Parson dropped his cigarette on the floor and smashed it under the slow pressure of his foot.

"Money," said the Parson, "is all that talks."

"How much money?" Jingo asked.

"Lend me a hundred dollars," said the Parson.

"Here you are, brother," answered Jingo, handing over the money.

"You've made a mistake and given me a hundred and twenty," said the Parson, pocketing the money. "That'll teach you to make your change more careful, in the future, kid. Now, before there's any betting, I wanna be honest. I wanna tell you something. You might think that Tower Creek has gone and hired an orchestra with two slide trombones in it for nothing. You're wrong. They hired it for Eugenia Tyrrel."

"Eugenia," said Jingo. "What a name *that* is."

"Wait a minute," went on the Parson. "They go and hire her a special orchestra, like that, and they send around special word that the sheriff is going to be standing near the door of the dance hall, and any gent that comes along with a whiskey breath is going to be kicked in the face and throwed out in the gutter where he belongs, the pup. You follow me?"

"I'm drifting right along with you," said Jingo.

"And the gents that get inside that dance hall all get special instructions that they ain't to mob the girl. They're to stand back and give her air. They ain't to ask her to dance with them unless the sheriff himself gives them an introduction. She's to be left to her three or four slick young Easterners. For why? Because it's a big honor for a Tyrrel to come into a dump of a town like this and look it over. Tower Creek is all heated up with joy because the girl has come down here for a frolic, if you follow me."

"I follow you so far," Jingo assured him, "that I begin to feel pain."

"You'll be eased of the pain when you see the girl," said the Parson.

"Is she the goods?" asked Jingo.

"She is the stuff," the Parson confirmed. "She is the horsehair bridle and the gold work on the saddle. She is the silk sash and the diamond pin."

"Well," Jingo said, sighing, "I can see, every minute, that I'm right at the age of retirement. I've got to go in and give that poor girl a whirl. Stand by, brother. When she's dizzy, I may lean her against you. Fan her and treat her right."

The Parson cleared his throat.

"I wouldn't go so far as to say that you mightn't take two steps with her in a tag dance, before the sheriff slams you into the street."

"Parson," said Jingo, "you are speaking to a man incapable of low devices and tricks."

"In that case," the Parson answered, "I've got a hundred dollars that says you won't dance a full dance with her."

"In that case," Jingo said, "I ought to give you odds. A hundred bucks it is."

"Jingo," said the Parson, "you're terrible young. But I got a soft place in my heart for kids, even the fool ones. Now put up your money or shut up."

Jingo put his money on the table. He said dreamily: "But she'll have to have a face, Parson. There's something more than money to be looked for in this short life of ours."

Chapter Six

There had been, long ago, a great, flourishing commercial enterprise started in Tower Creek. The idea was to cut thousands of tons of hay in the spring and store it in town through the winter, to be peddled at high prices to ranchmen whose cattle might be starving through the bad season. The enterprise had accomplished the building of the great barn and stopped there.

Tower Creek inherited the barn and used it for dances and major assemblies of all sorts. It was a big, crazy structure through which the wind whistled and whose walls wavered and rattled in a storm. But this night was still, hot, close. The lanterns that were strung along the walls and hung from the lower rafters increased the heat and gave to the air a grim savor, which mingled with the fragrance of talcum powders, and the acrid scent of alkali dust that somehow managed to work up through the cracks in the floor.

But it was a good dance. And all of Tower Creek was there, from the band on the platform at the far end to the ticket taker and the sheriff at the entrance door.

Almost all of Tower Creek had gathered before Jingo and the Parson took post under the big trees in front of the barn to see the arrival of the guests of honor.

Presently they came up in two rubber-tired buggies drawn by eager, dancing horses. Down from the buggies climbed three gentlemen in sharply creased white linen, and a girl all in white, also, with blue flowers pinned to her dress. The bystanders surged one half step toward her and stood rigid. Only Jingo did not move.

Afterward, the Parson turned toward him and gasped: "Well, kid, I'm sorry about the hundred dollars. But it's going to do me more good than it ever would do for you. Did you see 'em?"

"I saw her," said Jingo. "And I feel a little sad, Parson, when I see that I'll really have to retire from active life and start managing cattle ranches and gold mines, and things like that. I suppose I'll have to open an office on Wall Street to keep New York in order, now and then. Yes, Parson, the good old days are nearly over for Jingo, I fear."

"I'm not talking about her," the Parson said. "I told you she was a star. I was talking about the three beauties that come with her, all in white. Who'd ever think of dressing up in white, Jingo? Dog-gone, if they didn't even have on white shoes. And they had on white silk socks. I seen one of them socks as the bird was stepping out of the rig. Now wouldn't that beat Aunt Maria?"

"The fashions, Parson," said Jingo, "are things

you cannot be expected to understand. Your big, honest, simple nature cannot keep step with such frivolities. But . . . I hope the girl knows how to dance."

"Listen, Jingo," said the Parson, "are you going to shame me tonight? Are you going to be a plain fool and try to crash through and dance with that girl?"

"Before I get through," said Jingo, "you're going to open your blue eyes a great deal wider than they are just now. Stop holding your stomach, no matter how it aches, and tell me how I'm to get past that sheriff at the door, will you?"

"Sure," said the Parson. "Just step into your white linens, brother, and walk right in."

"Well," said Jingo, "I see that it's to be a matter of talking. Buy a pair of tickets, and you go first."

Accordingly the Parson bought the tickets, and strode for the door.

The sheriff looked him quickly up and down. Then he accepted the slip of pasteboard, saying as he did so: "You know Miss Tyrrel by sight? Then keep away from her till you're introduced. Savvy?"

The Parson nodded and stalked ahead.

"Hello, Sheriff," Jingo said, offering his ticket in turn.

"Hello, Jingo," said the sheriff, failing to notice the ticket apparently. "It's a mighty hot night, ain't it?"

"Out in the street," said Jingo. "But inside there, it looks as though a fellow could cool his eyes off a little."

"You're wrong, son," Sheriff Cary said. "That lantern light, in there, heats up the gents so that their reputations can be seen right away."

"That's good," said Jingo, "because I've nothing to be ashamed of."

"Sure you wouldn't be ashamed," said the sheriff. "But I never knew a gunfighter that didn't like himself pretty well. Back up, Jingo, and let the folks pass."

Jingo looked long and quietly into the eyes of the sheriff as he stepped aside.

The sheriff looked long and not so quietly back into the eyes of Jingo.

"You're not kind to yourself, Sheriff," said Jingo.

The sheriff stuck out his blunt jaw. He said: "Young feller, I've had plenty enough of your lip for one day. You can't threaten me. If I get another word out of you, I'll find you breaking the peace. Get away from this door and stop blocking the traffic."

Jingo looked past that angry face and saw, nearby, the long face and the twisting grin of the Parson. Music began to blare loudly. And far off, as the dancers swirled out onto the floor, he saw a girl in shimmering white swing away with a slender youth in shining linen.

Jingo turned and went back into the outer dark. Even Jingo's spirit, for that moment, began to shrink in his breast. And yet he was not thinking of the $100 that he had bet.

Chapter Seven

There were a lot of small boys scuffing up dust in the street, and bathing in the bright light that poured out of the entrance of the barn, and watching the late arrivals at the dance, and the dancers themselves who came out to wander up and down beneath the trees during the intervals. Something about one of those boys took the dreaming eye of Jingo as he strolled away. It was the red of the lad's hair. He was smaller than most of his companions, and his red hair stood up like that of a South Sea Island chief.

Jingo drew near and beckoned to the boy who came slowly and by a cautious and irregular line of approach, as one who knew that older men have heavy hands.

When he was near enough for Jingo to see the gleam of his eyes, Jingo said: "What do you know about a five-dollar bill?"

"I read a book that told about one, once," said the redhead.

"Here, Red." Jingo put a bank note in the boy's hand.

The youngster gave the bill one instant of examination, and then slipped it into a trousers pocket. He walked up to Jingo and stood at attention.

"You want another?" asked Jingo.

"I could eat 'em all day long," said Red.

"There's another waiting for you," Jingo told him. "But I want to tell you something first. There's a bowlegged, thick-headed sap standing in the door of that dance hall."

"Tell me his name," said Red, "and I'll go and chase him out."

"He's the sheriff," Jingo answered.

"He hit me on the seat of the pants with the workin' end of a black snake, one night," said Red. "I know my time would come."

"Where were you that night?" asked Jingo.

"I happened to be in his hen house, studyin' how nice the roosters looked in the moonlight," answered Red.

"Has the sheriff got a son?" Jingo asked.

"Yeah. And I can lick him."

"Have you licked him already?"

"I'm goin' to do it again, too," declared Red.

"What's his name?"

"Bobby. Which Bobby is a fool name, ain't it?"

"I never liked it," said Jingo. "You're going to run up to the door of the barn and tell the sheriff that something has happened to Bobby and he's got to come home at once."

Red shook his head.

"There ain't nothing can happen to Bobby," he answered. "He's got measles, and his ma doesn't do nothing but watch out for him all day long."

"All right," Jingo said. "He's got a relapse."

"What's a relapse?"

"It's a worse kind of measles. Run around this block as fast as you can leg it, and then go up to the sheriff and make your eyes big, and tell him the doctor's at his house, and his wife wants him, and Bobby has a relapse."

"I can tell him his house is on fire, too," suggested Red.

"You leave it the way I say."

"All right. That's the way it'll be."

"Wait a minute. Here's that other five dollars."

He passed it over as Red gasped: "Jiminy!"

"On your way," Jingo commanded.

The feet of Red made a whispering in the dust. His body, swaying with speed, dissolved into the blackness beneath the trees. And in a little while, a gasping, straining, desperate figure of Red dashed up to the barn entrance from the other side with wisps of dust whirling in the air behind him as he disappeared at the doorway.

A moment later, he came out again, and the sheriff appeared at once, striding big, swinging his body a bit to get more length in his steps. Jingo disappeared behind a tree.

When he stepped out again and went toward the entrance, he passed the small body and the red head of the boy as the youngster leaned against a tree.

"Go get her, cowboy," murmured Red.

Jingo laughed as he went forward, for he took this as an omen of good fortune.

When he came to the door, there was only the ticket taker to deal with. The ticket taker knew perfectly well that Jingo had been turned away once before, but he also knew what had happened to Wally Rankin in the back room of Slade's saloon. He knew a great deal about guns and what they could do, because he was a hardware dealer, so, when Jingo looked him firmly in the eye, he accepted the ticket without a single word.

Jingo walked through the doorway, saying: "Go take me over to Miss Tyrrel and tell her that the sheriff told you to introduce me to her. Understand? No loitering, either."

The hardware man blinked behind his glasses; his heart shrank small in his breast.

"But the sheriff *didn't* tell me to do that," he mourned.

"I'm telling you, and that's enough," Jingo said. "Come along."

The ticket taker obeyed, stepping on the edges of his feet as though he were afraid that he might make a noise, and yet the orchestra was doing its loudest best at the moment.

Along the edge of the dance floor, sometimes pausing to avoid the whirling dance couples, they journeyed together, not unnoticed, for little hushed gasps came from various of the girls and little humming sounds of surprise from the men, and the name, Jingo, was more than once in the air.

They all knew Jingo, it appeared. But then he was an expert in making himself known.

He said to the ticket taker: "My name is Jim Oreville. You got that?"

"Oreville. Oreville," muttered the hardware man rapidly. "Yeah, I'll remember."

The dance ended. The whirlpools of the dancers dissolved. Right toward a little bright cluster at one end of the room went Jingo and his wretched victim, who made moaning sounds deep in his throat.

"Don't act that way," cautioned Jingo. "I don't mind you sweating like a stuck pig, but I hate to hear you mourning like a cow with a calf that's been turned into veal. Buck up, stiffen your back, and remember that it'll soon be over. Here we are. Brace right up to her. Tell yourself that you're her granduncle and that she's got to be nice for fear you won't leave her a slice of the chicken farm. Here we are. Now act up."

Now, up to this moment, everything was going exactly as the sheriff had arranged. Nobody except the very best people in the town of Tower Creek had been able to come close to Eugenia Tyrrel. The sons and the daughters of the biggest miners and cattlemen and lumber kings had been able to enter the gracious presence, but none of them stayed very long. The three cool, white exquisites who set off Eugenia made the youths feel that their hair was too long, their trousers not creased, and their clothes out of shape. The girls felt that to be seen once in the bright light of Eugenia was to be looked down upon forever.

So there remained that bright, cool, pleasant grouping of white in the corner of the room with the darker eddies of the crowd withdrawn. Eugenia Tyrrel was having a chair placed for her by one of her attendants while another brought her a drink in a glass silvered over with cold, and a third occupied her almost royal ear with murmured conversation. And just at this moment the darkness of the crowd thrust a member right into the group, for there was the ticket taker, perspiring very freely and bowing with little jerks in front of Miss Tyrrel.

He said: "Miss Tyrrel, the sheriff asked me to introduce to you . . . while he was away . . . he asked me to introduce you to . . . to . . ."

The wretched wits of the hardware man began to give way. He had forgotten the name. Leadville was the only thing that he could think of. And therefore, in despair, he groaned out: "Asked me to introduce you to Jingo."

Then he fled and left Jingo to make the most of it. All the four were looking at him. The girl was saying, in the most incurious way, that she was happy to meet Jingo. One of the young men in white linen looked him up and down as though he were a horse.

"Maybe this is the town entertainer," he said.

He was a handsome young man. He was just the height of Jingo and he was almost as good-looking, except that he was as blond as Jingo was dark. He had a little golden mustache that shone in the light of the dance hall, and in fact there was a shimmering radiance like money that extended even to the clothes of the youth.

Jingo looked on him with a calm eye, the eye of a Jove at rest, but nevertheless he was gripping a flaming thunderbolt of wrath in the right hand.

These things had been said and observed in a second or so after the introduction, and Jingo said: "No, I'm not the town entertainer. But the sheriff thought you were perhaps a little bored, Miss Tyrrel. He told me to come over and do what I could. I see you have a chair and a drink and a fan. All I can offer you is a dance."

"That's rather good, too," said the man with the little golden mustache. And he ran the tips of his fingers over that mustache. For it was so new that he had not lost the first fervor of his love for it and could not help caressing it from time to time.

The girl was avoiding the invitation with easy skill.

"Thank you," she said. "I want you to know Wheeler Bent. This is George Staley . . . and Lincoln Waterson. Is your name really Jingo?"

Jingo acknowledged the introductions with a light, quick handshake all around. He was glad to know that the name of the fellow with the golden mustache was Wheeler Bent. Already in his mind he was making plays upon the word and thinking of various ways in which stronger wheels than that could be bent.

"It makes a story," Jingo said.

The girl looked at Jingo, and Jingo looked at the girl. She looked so closely that she could see that his eyes were brown. They both smiled at exactly the same instant.

"Do sit down and tell me," she said.

"It's like this," Jingo began, who had finished cursing the hardware maker to himself. "The name's made up of two initials and a final word."

"Really?" said the girl.

He sat down beside her. It was when Jingo sat down that people could really see him. Any man can stand up straight, and a good few even know how to hold their head and balance their weight, but not one man in ten million knows how to sit on a chair as though it were a throne from which a world of opportunity may be surveyed, or as though it were the back of a horse fit to leap over mountains. That was how Jingo sat, however, turning just a little toward Eugenia Tyrrel, but never too much.

"Yeah, really," Jingo said. "The J is for Jumbo. The I is for Igarone, and the last name is Ngo."

She said nothing. She sat still, and her eyes were still, too, but the light in them was quivering.

"Ngo," Jingo said, "is African for great chief or king . . . Igarone is a family name, and Jumbo is used something like sir in English."

He grinned at her, and she grinned back. It was not a smile at all.

"You don't have to tell me," she said. "I've been out in British East Africa and picked up some of the lingo."

"So you know that Ngo stands for king?"

"As far as I'm concerned, it may," said the girl.

They laughed together.

Mr. Wheeler Bent cleared his throat and moved to a position from which he silently commanded the attention of Eugenia Tyrrel—and failed to get it.

"What were you doing in Africa?" Jingo asked her. "Shooting?"

"Yes. Lions."

"English lions?" asked Jingo.

"No." She chuckled. "African."

"Did you get any?"

She held up one finger.

"That's what the headman said," she explained. "But the lion didn't drop till after he'd fired a second shot. You can make up your mind for yourself."

"I've made up my mind," Jingo said, "that if I give some money to the trombone players, they'd

64

let us hear the music of the strings, for the next dance."

"That's the very best idea," said Eugenia Tyrrel, "that I've heard this evening . . . bar one."

"What one is barred?" Jingo asked.

"The one about Ngo," said the girl.

"One can always learn little things," said Jingo. "Are we dancing the next dance?"

She cast one fleeting glance at the polished tips of his boots.

"I'd like to," she told him.

"Oh, I say, Gene," interrupted Wheeler Bent.

"I thought he might have something to say," Jingo said in one of those voices that travel just far enough to be indiscreet.

"Yes, Wheeler?" said the girl with the first shadow of a frown.

"Your next dance is taken," Wheeler Bent informed her. "Terribly sorry."

"Is it taken?" she asked, looking very straight at her chief escort.

"Yes," he assured her.

"Well," murmured Eugenia Tyrrel, "later on, Mister Ngo?"

"Name any dance you please," he said.

"I'll work over her program," Wheeler Bent said. "It may take a little arranging. You know how things are. You have this one, I think, George."

George Staley stepped gladly forward as the

65

trombones made the air shudder with their wide-lipped blast.

"Later," the girl said over the shoulder of George.

"Later," Jingo confirmed.

Then he saw a figure striding swiftly toward him, half wrecking dancing couples on the way. The figure was that of the sheriff.

Suddenly Jingo was aware of a window open beside him and was taken with a desire for the cool of the outer night. He stepped through that window. The ground was a dozen feet below. But he hung an instant by the tips of his fingers, and landed as lightly beneath as any cat.

Chapter Eight

As the sheriff made for him and he made for the window, Jingo was aware of one important object, and that was the enormous bulk of the Parson striding in the sheriff's rear, and pointing his great arm over the sheriff's shoulder. There was not the slightest doubt that the Parson intended to win the $100 bet even if he had to use means a little too rough, even if he had to lean his mighty elbow on the shoulder of the law.

It was rather the coming of the Parson than the approach of the sheriff that had decided Jingo to seek the cool of the outer night.

Now he sat on the stump of a tree in front of the barn where only the vaguest glimmerings of light reached through the shadows, but light half so strong would have been enough to set glowing the hair of the lad who now appeared before him.

"I thought you'd be home in bed, by now, Red," said Jingo.

"I knew you'd be needing me again," Red responded. "Ain't she a dandy?"

"Who?" asked Jingo absently.

"I climbed up to one of the windows and looked in and seen everything," the boy explained. "Ain't she a jim-dandy? It's lucky that you're rich, mister."

"Yeah, it's lucky that I'm rich," Jingo said a little sourly.

He lapsed into a long silence. When he looked up from it, a moment later, Red was still standing immobile before him.

"Do I believe what I see or am I cock-eyed?" Jingo asked. "Are those people that are arriving just now wearing masks?"

"I've been watching and thinking about it," Red said. "But it ain't no good. Every gent has to lift his mask for the sheriff to see him as he goes through the door."

"Are you sure?" insisted Jingo.

"Dead certain. I can see what they're doing from here."

"The devil," Jingo muttered.

"Take a new hand," Red said. "You ain't beat while you got money."

"Here's five dollars," Jingo said.

"What for?" Red asked, taking the money with a moist, swift hand.

"To do some thinking for me. Start thinking, and think fast. This dance won't last forever."

"Whatcha want?" asked the boy. "Her?"

"Yes," said Jingo.

"Are you going to fetch her away on your horse and marry her somewheres?" asked Red.

"I want to dance one whole dance with her," Jingo said.

"Oh, is that all?" Red asked with a note of deepest disappointment in his voice.

"That's all."

"Well, you're Jingo, ain't you? You got guns, ain't you? Why don't you go and shoot 'em up and dance all you wanna dance?" He added, in a greater disgust: "Dance? Huh."

"Listen, Red," Jingo urged. "Brain work is what I want. Not abuse."

"All right," Red said.

He sat down on the other side of the stump.

"She liked you," Red pondered aloud. "You didn't have long, but you made her shine."

"Did I?" asked Jingo sadly.

"Sure you did. Clean from the window where I was, I seen. I pretty near tasted the wedding cake."

After a time Red said: "If you had on some of them white clothes, like yonder, they might help."

"White clothes? Where?"

"See them white trousers walking, over there?"

Jingo could see them. The low-sweeping branches covered the upper part of the silhouette, but Jingo could see white trousers walking beside a white skirt. Suddenly he stood up.

"Red," he said, "I knew you had a brain. Now show that you've got eyes that can see in the dark. Just scatter along over there. See if the fellow walking with that white skirt is wearing a little yellow mustache . . . and see if the girl is my girl, will you?"

"What'll you do? Sock him?" Red asked eagerly.

"Go along and do what I say," said Jingo.

Red disappeared.

A moment later a whisper came out of the darkness, and Red was before him, panting.

"It's your girl, and it's the gent with the yaller mustache," declared Red.

Jingo bent back his head and looked at the bright stars in the sky. And every one of them smiled at him.

"Now listen," he said. "But first, hold out your hand."

"My thunder," Red muttered. "Another?"

"If I had a million, I'd give you half," Jingo answered heartily. "You barge up to those two . . . Wait a minute . . ."

"It's hard to wait, but I'll do it," said Red.

"What are those masks for?"

"Everybody's going to put on masks to jollify things up a little at twelve o'clock. It ain't minus twelve more'n five minutes now. The grand noise is going to start," declared Red.

"It is," Jingo said gently. "The grand noise *is* about to start." He went on: "Run up to them . . . tell them . . . call him Mister Bent. Understand?"

"I could understand anything, just now," Red said with pride. "All right. His name is Mister Bent . . . and your name is Jingo."

"Leave my name out of it. Run up to him and

say . . . 'Mister Bent, I've been looking for you everywhere. The buggy horses got into a ruction, and your near horse has been kicked and is down.' Understand? Tell him to come quick."

"Suppose," Red said, "that your girl goes along with him?"

"That would be the devil. But we've got to chance it. Wait here while you count sixty. Then start. You know where the horse sheds are?"

"Sure I know where they are."

"Well, then, if you can get him away from the girl, whistle as you come along with him. If you can't get him away from the girl, you'd better fade out into the dark."

"I will," said Red. "I'll do everything . . . and his name is Bent."

It was only a part of a minute after this that strange things began to happen to Wheeler Bent. As he walked up and down with Eugenia Tyrrel on his arm, a little red-headed boy rushed up to them out of the shadows.

He called: "Mister Bent? Mister Bent?"

"Here, my lad," Wheeler Bent said.

The boy danced on one foot, pointing away.

"Back yonder . . . the horses been in a ruction. Your near horse was knocked flat. They want you to come along quick to see . . ."

"I'll go with you," the girl said, swaying forward, ready to run.

That was the trouble with her. Even if she were

Missus Wheeler Bent, she would still be ready to pick up her skirts and run like a boy. She would still be ready to climb a tree. And this beautiful, gay, rash, reckless thing was entrusted chiefly to his guardianship tonight. It might be that he would be tempted to extend his authority over her to a greater time and on a stronger basis.

He said: "Stay here, Gene. Go right back into the dance room, please. You don't want to be mixed up with a lot of sweating, kicking, dusty horses. Go back, please."

She went back. She only gave to him one rather vague glance that drifted away and was lost among the shadows or the stars. Wheeler Bent could not tell which. As soon as he saw her safely started toward the wedge of bright light that seemed to flow in from the dusty night, instead of issuing from the interior of the barn, Bent went after the boy.

He did not run. He was a powerful fellow, was Wheeler Bent, and every inch of his trim body was layered and lined with strings of muscle, such as constant athletics give to a man. He was as good a runner as one could have found in a county, but he had a very nice sense of the fitness of things and he was not one to run on account of a carriage horse. For a thoroughbred? Well, perhaps. But Wheeler Bent believed that there should be a decent proportion between the needs of life and the actions that serve them. So he merely went forward at a good brisk walking gait with the branches of the big trees moving back above his head until he was in a thickness of gloom.

Then he saw a man who appeared suddenly, as though he had just stepped from behind a tree trunk.

"Mister Bent?" said the stranger.

"Well?" Bent said curtly. Then he recognized Jingo and instantly realized his scheme. "You!" And in a swift flare of anger he aimed a hasty, uncalculated punch at Jingo.

"Well enough," Jingo said, dodging, and then he hit Wheeler Bent right on the point of the chin. The shock, of course, seemed to fall on the base of Wheeler Bent's brain. His knees and all his body sagged forward to meet the twin brother of that first punch that turned the dark of the night into one great flower of red, then all light ceased in the brain of Wheeler Bent.

Chapter Nine

When Wheeler Bent recovered, he was lying in the dust in his fine linen underwear. Even his shoes and his socks were gone. His hands were tied behind his back, and the same rope passed around the trunk of a tree. Furthermore, there was a tightly twisted roll of cloth in his mouth that served to gag him, so that he could only make a dull, moaning sound.

He sat up. The shadows spun around and around. Finally he was able to rise, though the pull of the rope kept him bowed low. Figures, now and then, moved in the near distance, and he strove to attract attention by making gestures with his feet and by uttering the highest-pitched moan of which he was capable.

But while the people trooped calmly back toward the lighted entrance, not far away, and while the strains of the dance music began with unusual gentleness—for the trombones were altogether silent—it seemed to Wheeler Bent that he was going to be allowed to strangle unheeded in the darkness of the night. It was not the gag but the fact that he was unheeded that was strangling Wheeler Bent.

Then there appeared, close to him, a strolling group of the bare-footed urchins of the town. They were startled, at first, by the queer sounds he made, and by the whiteness of his form in the night. But when they had had a chance to examine him more closely, they began to yell with delight.

Boys have the souls of savages with a sense of humor added, and it seemed to that cluster that here was the victim of a practical joke given into their hands.

They untied one end of the rope from around the tree, but they kept the other end hitched to the wrists of Wheeler Bent. When he tried to break away, half a dozen of the youngsters attached themselves to the rope and hauled him back. When he tried to charge in at them, they threw clever little loops of the rope that caught him by the feet.

To fall without hands to save one is not pleasant, and after a time Wheeler Bent stopped charging so furiously. Those lads kept him like a live bear on the end of that rope and swept around him in circles. Their ringleader, their inspiring genius, was a red-headed youngster half the size and twice the devilishness of his companions. It was he who pointed out the glimmering, golden mustache of Wheeler Bent—and straightaway tarnished the mustache with dust. They went on and tarnished all of Mr. Bent with dust.

He was sweating profusely; his outraged spirit was literally breaking out through the pores of his skin. Therefore the dust clung and turned him from a cool, white form to an almost black one. The more outrageous his appearance became, the more those lads yelled with delight and whirled about like the vortex of a tornado.

He was at the point of choking with rage when, luckily, he managed to spit the gag out of his mouth. He took one deep breath, and then he let out a yell that whistled through his teeth and tore at his vocal chords. He kept right on yelling. He threatened to have the lot of them in a reform school before morning.

He yelled so loudly that worse things began to happen to him. The last event that the sheriff wanted was the attendance of any drunken loiterers who might make a disturbance outside the barn while the dance was in progress. In order that Tower Creek might continue to put forward its best foot without annoyance, the sheriff posted his most-trusted deputy, Steve Matthews, outside the barn.

Matthews was a man small of speech and large of hand. When he heard the furious whoop of Wheeler Bent, he went straight for the scene of action. He saw the wheeling circles of the boys. He saw the rope. He saw the man in underwear. And Steve Matthews blushed not with shame but with anger.

Suppose that the eyes of some of the ladies had fallen on this grotesque?

He was glad he had gloves on his hands when he

went in and took the rope out of the hands of the boys. They scattered with yells of fresh pleasure when they saw the law taking up where they had left off.

Wheeler Bent yelled: "Arrest those little ruffians . . . arrest those young hyenas . . . those . . . !"

The gloved hand of Steve Matthews was clapped over the mouth of his victim. It was a good, thick, buckskin glove, and yet he was somewhat afraid that the fellow might bite through the leather into his flesh.

"You fool of a drunk half-wit," said the deputy, "shut up your mug and march along with me."

"I'm Wheeler Bent!" shouted the captive.

"You'll be a plumb broke wheel if you don't shut up," declared the deputy. "I gotta mind to sock you."

"He's Wheeler Bent! He's Wheeler Bent!" chanted the red-headed boy, and all the rest of the evil little tribe took up the cry, exploding with laughter.

And Wheeler Bent, assuring himself that he was going mad, found himself dragged down the street behind his tall captor.

They came to a little squat building with the fatal bars across the windows. The door was opened. They passed in. A Negro came carrying a big bunch of keys. A cell was opened, and Wheeler Bent actually found himself in jail.

"Disturbing the peace is the charge ag'in' you,"

the deputy said calmly. "And if you don't get three months, I'm a sucker, and the judge is a worse one. What you been drinking? I didn't get it on your breath."

A hoarse, trembling voice came out of the throat of Wheeler Bent.

He said: "You're going to be smashed, for this. If Judge Tyrrel has any influence in this part of the country, you're going to be smashed flat. Robbery and assault right in the middle of the town."

There was only one thing in this speech that meant anything to the deputy, and that was the name of Judge Tyrrel. It was true that the judge resided, when in the West, in Blue Water, but his hand was strong even farther away than Tower Creek.

Steve Matthews, therefore, narrowed his eyes and considered his prisoner a little more closely.

"Hey, George," he said to the Negro, "go fetch a bucket and sluice off this gent. We'll have a look at him."

The water was brought, a three-gallon pail full of it, and it was doused suddenly over the head and the entire body of Wheeler Bent.

To him, this was the greatest outrage of all. It left him rigid with rage, like molten steel when it is suddenly cooled. And he wished that death might suddenly sweep the town of Tower Creek.

But what the deputy sheriff saw, first and last and all the time, was the gleaming little golden mustache that adorned the upper lip of his prisoner. He had seen that before, and he had seen only one like it, and it was worn by the dapper youth who had been the chief escort of the Tyrrel girl.

A sudden shadow swept over the brain of Matthews. He took a quick, deep breath and stared again.

"By the leaping thunder," he said. "George, get the door of that cell open, because it appears to me like maybe we've started more trouble popping than we knew anything about."

Chapter Ten

Not long before, Jingo had finished stripping and re-dressing himself. Now he looked down with satisfaction on the white gleam of his borrowed suit. The little red flower at the buttonhole of the left lapel had been more than a bit crushed, but when he dusted it off, it looked fresh enough to pass. He felt that he might need that red flower as the final token of his new identity. Then he took from a pocket a light hood of white silk that went completely over his head. The care of Wheeler Bent for detail had been so exact that he had even furnished his mask with a curling red feather that trembled along one side of it.

Best of all, the clothes fitted. Even the shoes were exactly the right size—a thing that caused Jingo to feel a sudden accession of respect for his late enemy.

Then he went into the barn.

The hardware merchant was there at the door. So was the sheriff. And in the near distance, none other than the lofty form of the Parson could be seen, towering above his neighbors. He had picked out the smallest and the most-freckled girl in the crowd, and the mask that he was wearing was not half big enough to cover his smile.

"Here's Mister Wheeler Bent," said the hardware man.

"Hello, Mister Bent," said the sheriff.

Jingo waved an airy hand and walked through the gate into the interior. He had a little time on his hands, but not too much. For he could not tell when Wheeler Bent would rouse and get help. And by the exactness with which the borrowed clothes fitted him, Jingo could prophesy the hugeness of the wrath of Wheeler Bent.

The dance was about to commence.

He drifted by the half-masked giant, the Parson, saying: "Oh, just a moment, if you please."

The Parson turned slowly toward him and made a partial step. If the mask could not cover all his smile, it could not begin to cope with his scowl, and now he was scowling.

"Well?" growled the Parson.

Jingo spoke in his natural voice.

He said: "I'm about to start dancing with her, Parson. If you try to double-cross me again, I'll knock so many holes through you that your black heart'll come out to surprise the world."

The Parson was made into a rigid form, by this announcement. And leaving him transfixed, Jingo went on to win something more than the $100 that he had wagered.

He found the cool little pool of white in the farther corner. The two young men gave Jingo a bit of applause for the handsome quality of his hood, which had quite undone them. He merely waved his hand at them and murmured to the girl: "This dance is ours?"

When she heard his voice, she looked up at him quickly, and he saw her eyes open and close as swiftly as the shutter of a camera. He knew that the idea was safely enclosed in her mind in that instant.

She stood up. The orchestra was beginning to tune. Jingo took note of the black mask that covered her face down almost to the tip of the nose. As though her smile in itself were not sufficiently revealing! Merely the blue stain of her eyes, he felt, would have been enough for him to identify her.

"Let's go by the orchestra and see if I can persuade the slide trombones to rest their arms," Jingo said.

She looked up and aside at him, once more, and went along without a word. And his heart jumped. She was able to do her thinking in silence, and her price mounted suddenly in his estimation.

So he went on to the orchestra and slipped a $5 bill into the good right hand of each of the trombone players.

"Miss Tyrrel has a frightful headache," Jingo told each. "Perhaps you'd better not play this one dance."

Said the older of the two artists: "Sure. I know. We'll just kind of let the old trombones mourn along with the rest of the music. It wouldn't sound like no real orchestra without no trombones in it."

"Chance it just this once," Jingo said. "I'm only speaking for the lady."

He went to the orchestra leader and gave him two of those $5 bills.

"You're putting on a great show, brother," said Jingo. "But the trombones could rest, one dance. Miss Tyrrel has a headache."

"So have I," the orchestra leader said. "I've had the things blatting and blubbering in my ears all evening long. If I had my way, all the trombone trumpets would be stuffed down the throats of the brass-headed fools that play 'em."

A sudden smile came in the eyes of Jingo. He took his likes even as his dislikes—on the wing. And he liked that orchestra leader.

He turned back to the girl as the music commenced with the swaying rhythm of a waltz. And that was why wretched Wheeler Bent, when bound and gagged, had heard the orchestra strike up without the braying of the slide trombones.

"What has become of Wheeler Bent?" she asked breathlessly. "What have you done to him?"

"Not a hair of his head has been hurt," said Jingo.

"No, but every bone in his body might be broken," she suggested.

"Where's the woman's instinct?" asked Jingo.

"That is my instinct," she said.

"The only thing that's wrong with him now," he said, "is that he's choking with anger. It's as big as a fist in his throat."

"He hasn't come to harm?"

"You know he hasn't. You're dancing here with me."

"Jingo, who are you?"

"I'm the town entertainer," he told her.

"Was *that* why you've done some terrible thing to Wheeler Bent?"

"I've only given him a chance to do a little quiet thinking. He'll be able to forget his bright little mustache and look at Nature, Gene."

He felt the flash of her eyes as she looked swiftly up at him.

"The great big mountains of the open-hearted West, Gene," he said, persisting in the nickname calmly, "they're good for any man, and if they can cure a sore heart, I don't see why they can't cure a sore jaw."

The music rose into a fine sweep now, and they gave themselves up to it. He danced like a silky stepping Mexican. They went through a group of the dancers without touching a sleeve.

"I've got to go to poor Wheeler," the girl said.

"You'd better let the mountain come to Mahomet," said Jingo.

"Are you going to tell me what you did to him?"

"I sent a red-headed boy to tell him that one of his horses was down. Then I met him on the way and tapped him on the chin and took his clothes and tied him to a tree. How much do you mind?"

She began to laugh, even while she was shaking her head.

"It will kill Wheeler," she said. She almost stopped in the dance. "He'll know that I've danced with a stranger dressed in his clothes," she cried breathlessly.

"He will," Jingo agreed. "That's what makes it perfect."

"Perfect?" she asked.

"A perfect scandal," Jingo elaborated. "Your father will have to know. And just as you start to forget about everything that happened in Tower Creek, they'll start in reminding you. I don't want you to forget me before I come to call on you."

"Are you coming to call? Are you coming up to Blue Water to call?" she asked.

"If they hired all the United States Army and marched it in ranks around your father's house, I'd find a way through 'em," Jingo said cheerfully and confidently. "Unless you tell me not to come."

"You must not come!" she cried.

"All right then," Jingo said. "I won't."

"But I want you to," added the girl. "But you mustn't."

"If you want me to, I'll be there."

"I'd be in a real terror," she said.

But she had begun to laugh again, quietly.

"When shall I come?" asked Jingo.

"I'm going back home tomorrow. Suppose you come in the twilight of the day?"

"Certainly," Jingo said. "Tell your father that I'm coming, will you?"

"Tell him? You don't know my father. He's a very stern man, Jingo. He's a frightfully stern man. I don't know what he'd do."

"He'll call out the foot and horse," Jingo said, "and that will make the game."

"You actually mean that I'm to tell him?"

"Of course you are. We don't want to do anything underhanded, do we?"

She looked straight up at him, without her laughter now.

"Will you tell me who you are?" she asked.

"I'm a traveler," said Jingo.

"Where do you travel?"

"Oh, from place to place."

"But how do you live?"

"On the best in the land."

"I don't mean that."

"How do I make money? Well, I play a pretty good game of cards. I generally have a horse fast enough to get inside the money at the rodeo races. And one way and another I get along very well."

She was silent.

"Someday I may find something worth doing," Jingo said.

"Will you tell me your real name?" she asked.

"I've taken an oath," said Jingo, "never to tell a

soul except the woman who marries me, if I ever find one."

The music rose to a crescendo, and then died out to a sudden halt. They walked side-by-side right past the vast shoulders and the staring eyes of the Parson.

"I'd better go," Jingo said. "Wheeler Bent may be awake, by this time, and in a short while he'll remember that there's a dance and that he needs clothes to go to it. Good bye."

"Are you going? First . . . of course it was only a joke . . . about your coming to Blue Water."

"No joke to me," said Jingo. "And I'll be there. Tomorrow at twilight. Before the sunlight's gone from the sky."

He left her at her chair, and went rapidly out of the room. The Parson, seeing a significant sign, had started to follow him, but before he reached the door, he was stopped for an instant by the entrance of the deputy sheriff.

Deputy Steve Matthews cried out: "Sheriff, have you seen a gent here dressed up in the clothes of Wheeler Bent? There's been assault and robbery around here."

"By the leaping thunder!" exclaimed the sheriff. "Then I know who did the job!"

Chapter Eleven

The excitement brought every man out of the dance hall in one rush. They poured here and there under the trees, looking for a fellow in the glimmering white of a linen suit, and they carried lanterns in their search, but no one climbed to the top of the horse shed, where Jingo was calmly seated, changing his clothes back to his own comfortable outfit.

When the tide had poured back into the barn, Jingo descended, put the linen suit in the fork of a tree, the shoes on top of the suit, and the wallet on top of the shoes, and went back toward the hotel. He only paused a moment at the door of the barn to look in.

He said: "Well, Sheriff, keeping everything in order?"

The sheriff looked at him with eyes that bulged with wrath.

"Jingo," he said in a trembling voice, "there's no way I can prove anything, but I'm going to make Tower Creek a hot griddle under you, you jumping flea."

Jingo laughed and went on to the hotel, where he found the Parson waiting for him. The $10 bills were lying in a pile on the center table. Jingo pocketed them without a word.

"Where do we head for?" asked the Parson.

"You guess," Jingo said.

"For trouble," said the Parson.

"What's the name of it, then?" asked Jingo.

"The name is Eugenia Tyrrel," the Parson said.

"We ride up to call on her tomorrow," agreed Jingo. "Be ready for the start, Parson."

"Old blue-eyed lightning," murmured the Parson. "I seen you strike Jingo in the middle of things."

It was only a little later than this that Wheeler Bent, again clothed in his white linen suit, confronted Eugenia Tyrrel. He was white about the mouth and red around the cheeks. His mouth worked so that his mustache bristled.

"My clothes," he stammered. "He had on my clothes. You couldn't fail to know them. They say . . . they say that incredible . . . the ruffian . . . that he even had the red flower in the buttonhole . . . and yet . . . and yet you actually danced with him. As if you didn't care. As if it didn't matter."

"I'm sorry, Wheeler," said the girl. "Is that purple spot on the chin where he hit you? Did he hurt you very much?"

Wheeler Bent caught in a breath. He looked straight into her eyes. He was on the very verge of believing that she was making light of Wheeler Bent. But then he realized that this could hardly be.

"I'm going crazy, Gene," he told her. "I'm losing my mind. *Why* didn't you call the sheriff the moment you understood . . . ?"

"I thought it was all just a joke," said the girl. "Are you sure that it was anything more?"

"Joke?" gasped Wheeler Bent. "He's a gunman. A notorious ruffian. A gambler. A saloon gambler. An idle tramp. He's knocked me out, and he's taken my clothes, and actually danced with you. Eugenia, he had his arm around you. What will your father say? And you call it a joke. . . . I've been assaulted, robbed, stripped, thrown into the common jail . . ."

He threw his hands up over his head. He kept one hand raised. He dropped the other and gripped his hair with it.

Eugenia Tyrrel said nothing. Her blue eyes were open and calm. She kept shaking her head and murmuring small words of sympathy, but nothing dimmed her eyes. They remained bright and curious.

Finally Wheeler Bent controlled himself. He looked at the girl, and all he could see was the blue of her eyes, not the lack of sympathy in them.

He exclaimed: "And they can't prove anything! Not unless they dragged you in for a witness. You're the only one that could prove that he was the assailant and the robber."

She was silent for a moment. "Did he keep your purse, Wheeler?" she asked at last.

"No, but the point is . . . ."

Suddenly he mastered himself, for something told him that he had been losing a great deal of ground in the last few moments. He gathered his dignity about him like a robe.

"One thing, at least," he said. "Your father must not know about this. I shall see that he never hears a word."

"He can't help hearing about it," answered the girl. "The gossip will surely reach him. Before it does, I intend to tell him myself. Besides, he has to know that Jingo intends to call on me tomorrow evening, at twilight."

"Jingo intends to . . . what?" Wheeler Bent cried.

"He says that he's coming to call on me before the end of tomorrow, in Blue Water," said Eugenia Tyrrel.

"The infernal ruffian!" cried Wheeler Bent.

"He's something more than that," the girl answered.

With that he stared at her, and saw that she at least meant all that she had said. He was by no means a fool. It was plain that he needed a bit of time for thinking, so he left her at once and went off to his room.

There he sat, with his chin on his fist, for a long time, pondering.

He had been playing for very high stakes when he was playing for Eugenia Tyrrel. He had a tidy little fortune of his own, but to get his hands on the Tyrrel millions would be to make himself one of the powerful ones of the world, he felt.

His bruised jaw began to thrust out a little farther. And his rather pale eye brightened and hardened.

He was remembering the house that had been pointed out as they drove into Tower Creek, the house where lived the hardest men in Tower Creek—gamblers and gunmen—the Rankin brothers.

Well, he had heard a good deal more about them in the course of the day and the evening. That had been only natural, for Tower Creek was humming with talk about the gunfight in which one of the Rankin brothers had gone down.

"Jake will level the score," everyone said. "Wally has the size, but Jake is the pure steel. He'll fix Jingo before he's through. Jingo has a smart way with a gun, but Jake will handle him, all right."

That was the way they had talked, and the more Wheeler Bent pondered the thing, the more he felt that he was called to see Jake Rankin and make somewhat more sure of the future. In short, he did not like the thing that had been in the eyes and in the voice of Eugenia Tyrrel when she had announced that Jingo intended to call at her home in Blue Water before the end of the next day.

Women like handsome youths.

At that thought he picked a lamp off the table and went to the mirror and held it over his head. The face that it showed him was handsome enough, he felt. It had given him a great many successes with the ladies, and, before the end, it ought to give him a great many more. There were only two defects in that face so far as he could see. One was a bruise on the right side of the chin, and one was a bruise on the left side of the chin, put there by the fists of a fellow whose face had a certain dark handsomeness that might be more pleasing, perhaps, to the eyes of a girl like Eugenia Tyrrel.

Not permanently. No, he could be sure that in the long run she belonged to him. But for the moment, Jingo might very well sweep her off her feet. And once she was swept away, might she not be taken to an irrecoverable distance?

The more he considered this, the darker became his thoughts.

Suddenly he was on his feet, his hat on his head, and a gray duster coat over his clothes. He went out on the street and down it until he reached the house of the Rankin brothers.

There was no light in the front of it. Down the side he saw one glimmer, and, going to the spot, through a broken shutter he saw an old, hard-faced woman asleep in a chair beside a bed. In the bed lay a man of gigantic torso, his shoulders and arms swathed in bandages.

It was highly necessary that Wheeler Bent should be seen by only one member of that household. He went down to the next window. It was open on darkness. He could lean in across the low window sill, and therefore he did so, and raised the thinnest of whistles.

Instantly it was answered by a rustling of bedclothes. A footfall pressed the floor with a sense of weight rather than a sound.

Then, not far from Bent, a voice murmured: "Well? What's up?"

"I want to talk to you on the quiet."

"Go back to the woodshed. There's a lantern inside it. Light that. I'll get there as soon as I've put on some clothes."

Bent pulled his head out of the darkness, feeling as though he had leaned into a wolf's cave where the brute lay asleep, but with senses attuned to the first warning whisper.

Behind the house, Bent found the shed, the door sagging open. He lit a match. From the cup of his hand he threw the light over the heap of stove wood, and over the dusty glimmer of the spider webs, like old, sagging sails. The gray of them filled the space between the rafters. Then the light glinted on the chimney of a lantern, which he set going.

He had hardly hung the lantern back on the wall before a man of more than middle size, his flannel shirt well filled with a padding of muscles, his face like the heavy-jawed but jointed face of a wolf, stepped through the doorway and looked silently at him.

A chill sprang out of the ground and ran trembling up the spinal column of Wheeler Bent.

"My name is Wheeler Bent," he said.

The stranger nodded and said nothing. It was as though he felt that it would be foolish to mention his own name, as though the entire world must know that he was Jake Rankin.

"And you're Jake Rankin?" asked Wheeler Bent.

Rankin nodded again. His jaw muscles were working a little. His eyes were working, also.

"I've come here to talk business with you," Wheeler Bent said.

Then, as his host nodded again, a sort of breathless despair came over Bent.

He said: "You want the scalp of Jingo, so do I."

At this Rankin grinned suddenly. It made his face even more formidable than before.

"I heard about things that happened at the dance," he said. "I heard that Jingo might've been there. Nobody else would've had the nerve, I guess."

His voice was rather high, but it was also husky. He sounded as though he could sing a loud and brazen tenor. When he had finished speaking, his jaws continued to work a little, as though he were masticating the last of a mouthful.

"They don't come in parcels . . . not gents like Jingo," he said.

"You like him?" Wheeler Bent asked, amazed.

Rankin looked away in thought.

"I dunno," he said at last. "I been around a good bit, and I've seen a lot of folks, but I dunno that I ever clapped my eyes on anybody that I ever liked as well as I like Jingo."

All the wind went out of Wheeler Bent as he answered: "Well . . . that's all right, then."

"Sure, it's all right. Who said that it wasn't all right?"

"Nobody," answered Bent. "Only I thought . . . I thought that you were after his scalp."

"Sure I am," Rankin answered calmly. "That's all right, too. I want his scalp, and I'm going to get it, but there's going to be a big red spot on the trail when the pair of us meet. What's your slice in the game?"

"I want to know when you start on the trail."

"Not now. My kid brother is all bashed up. Jingo done the bashing, and that's why I'm going to get Jingo. But I gotta stay here on the job. I gotta keep the meat in the pantry and help around the house till Wally is straightened out . . . as straight as he's ever going to be again."

"That's where I come in. I give you enough cash to fix you and the family."

"That's where you come in, is it? What would you call fixing?"

"You know what money you need for y_
family. I'll give you that much, and then you'_
free for the trail."

"I'd want a thousand," Rankin declared,
narrowing his eyes as he entered upon the
bargaining.

"A thousand would be all right," declared
Wheeler Bent.

"There's other expenses," Rankin continued.

"What are they? I thought you simply wanted to
be free."

"Jingo is traveling with a big whale of a gent
called the Parson. A gent that could eat a feller like
you or me at a coupla meals. I'd need a couple of
good men to cancel the Parson. I'd need to hire
'em."

"What would they cost?" Wheeler Bent asked
nervously.

"I dunno. Maybe another thousand apiece."

"That makes three thousand altogether!"
exclaimed Bent.

"No. Not altogether. There's the cost of three
good horses, too. And there's saddles and fixings,
all around, and a margin to work on. It'd come to
around about five thousand."

Bent groaned.

"It's too much. It's robbery," he announced.

"It's not robbery. It's murder."

Bent started. But there was plenty of metal in
him. And he kept thinking of the strange, new

light that had come glimmering into the eyes of the girl when she had spoken of young Jingo.

Rankin went on, explaining: "Nobody would be fool enough to hit the trail of Jingo and the Parson unless there was good money in it. Jingo ain't been in town a whole day, but he's gone and built himself a pretty tidy little reputation. Understand? I'd want to pick my men first. And afterward I'd want to be able to pay 'em what they ask. Suppose one of those gents wanted two or three thousand . . . I'd be out of luck, wouldn't I? No, I'm making it cheap when I say five thousand. Eight or ten thousand would be more like it."

Wheeler Bent looked through the blackness of the door. His mind took a hop, skip, and jump, and suddenly he pulled out the wallet that had been once in the hands of Jingo that night, but which had remained unopened.

"I have two thousand here that I can give you," he said. "Will you trust me for the rest . . . when the job's done?"

"Trust you?" Jake Rankin said. "Man, of course I'll trust you. You wouldn't run out on an honest debt to old Jake Rankin, I guess."

And his narrow mouth parted, and Bent watched the flash of his teeth as he laughed.

Chapter Twelve

Judge Tyrrel had filled his mind with a good many different interests, but to the end he retained the essential character of a cattleman. He had begun his life riding range, and he hoped to end his days on the range, also. Often he had to be away from his ranch for months at a time, but he always tried to get out into the hills at this season, when hay was being hauled in to fill the big barns and assure a supply of winter feed for the stock.

In some of his other activities he had to dress and talk politely. But when he was on his ranch, he liked to let everything slip. Even his house was more barn than dwelling. He had built four big barns, end to end, and just when he finished building them, the rickety old ranch house burned down. Another man of the judge's wealth would have seized on the occasion to work out with a good architect the plans for a great mansion in the hills, but the judge was a practical fellow, and he hated show.

Therefore, since by stowing away the hay carefully, three barns could be made to serve in the place of four, he had the fourth altered a bit to make it into a house. The ends of the building were chopped up into box-like rooms, three stories of them. The central part of the great mow was left open. It made the living room, the dining room, the assembly hall of the house. The floor of it was simply the compacted earth. Ranges of intercrossing, unpainted tie beams and struts filled the gloom with confusion overhead when lamps were lit of an evening, and there was a great fireplace built against one wall in which whole logs could be consumed.

The more polite of the judge's friends were a bit shocked when they were brought into such a living room, but it exactly pleased the judge.

Better than the house, he liked the saddle. When he had ranged over the wide miles of the ranch through the day, almost best of all he enjoyed some time at the end of the day sitting under the enormous spruce that grew in front of his barn house. Usually those huge trees are found in twos and threes near some creek, standing in the midst of a forest that shrinks back from the regal presence, but this giant stood by itself, drooping its branches of tufted silver-blue. Judge Tyrrel had a good friend and a daughter he loved, but nothing in the world was in his thoughts as often as the great silver spruce at Blue Water. And as he sat in a canvas chair under the vast branches on this afternoon, he felt that the tree was aware of him, as he was aware of the tree.

He could sit at the head of a long table, surrounded by important directors, and never be aware of half the power that was his as he lounged in the canvas chair under the great Colorado spruce. For many years ago he had gripped the bare sides of his mustang with his bare legs, and looked at the tree, and listened to the talking of the creek, and told himself that one day his ranch house would stand on the spot. That was why the place was dream-like to him. All that he saw from his chair fitted into the vision, from the mountains, huddled into their forests as into ragged furs, with shining white mantles over their heads and shoulders, to the distant town of Blue Water, which was vainly trying to make an important smoke in the lower valley.

The face of the judge remained smooth and young, although he was just sixty. But the weight of a great, pyramidal brow bent his head continually forward and showed the sparseness of the silvering hair. His neck was growing thin, also, and even the thickness of his flannel shirt could not cover up the boniness of his shoulders. He had a bandanna around his throat, blue jeans on his legs, and high-heeled range boots on his feet. He looked like a cowpuncher well over his years of efficient labor, and ready to retire to days of ease.

As he sat in the canvas chair, he used the keen edge of his pocket knife to pare away thin, translucent shavings from a stick of soft pine. Now and then he lifted his weighty brow and looked at the mountains, or at the glimmering windows of Blue Water. Now and then he gave a glance to the two people near him, his daughter and young Wheeler Bent. She sat cross-legged, with her back against the vast brown knuckle of a root of the tree, which broke out from the ground.

But Wheeler Bent was standing for two reasons. One was that he thought his golden hair and golden mustache looked their best with a background of blue sky to set them off. The more important reason was that Wheeler Bent was about to be noble, and anyone knows that it is better to be standing straight when on a noble stage.

Judge Tyrrel said: "Now, tell me, what about all this?"

"Go on, Father," said the girl. "All what?"

"Wheeler," he demanded, without lifting his eyes from his whittling, "did Gene carry on and make a fool of herself with a young feller down there in Tower Creek?"

When the judge came to his ranch, he put formal language and formal grammar as far from him as he put formal clothes. He made himself easy in his speech.

Wheeler Bent lifted his golden head a little higher.

"Of course not," he said. "Eugenia couldn't."

"Couldn't what?" asked the judge.

"Couldn't make a . . . ," stammered Wheeler Bent, "couldn't make a . . . a fool of herself."

"Couldn't she?" asked the judge.

"She is your daughter, sir," said Wheeler Bent.

"Wheeler," said the judge, "I've been a fool most of my days, and when I was her age I was the greatest fool in the world. I was worth traveling to see, I was such a big fool. You could've called me Old Faithful, I was a fool so regular and so often."

He shook his glorious head and went on with his whittling.

The girl said nothing. She had her bare, brown elbow resting on her knee, and her brown chin was cupped in her hand as she turned her head a little from the young man to her father, watching. The great spruce shed its fragrance over her and allowed golden handfuls of sunshine to slip through its branches and spill over her continually. There was a moment of silence, in which the speaking of the creek seemed to grow louder and to approach them with its presence.

"You, speaking personal and for yourself," said the judge, "haven't anything to complain about down there in Tower Creek, Wheeler? Nothing you could say against Gene?"

The young man lifted his head higher still. He wanted his pose to be remembered. For this was his chance to be his noblest, and he wanted to take advantage of it.

"No, sir," he said. "I haven't a word to say against Gene . . . of course not."

The judge lifted his head for half a second.

"Well, well, well," he said. "I didn't think it was

as bad as that. I didn't think she'd been so bad that her friends had to lie about her. Gene, stand up here."

"I'd rather take it sitting," said Eugenia Tyrrel.

"You're a lazy young loafer," said the judge, holding out for his own admiration a transparent shaving half a yard in length. "You're a lazy, spoiled, random young whippersnapper, Gene."

"I ought to be pitied," said the girl. "I've been spoiled. Only children always ought to be pitied. I read that in a book somewhere."

"Spanking is better for them than pitying," said the judge.

He looked suddenly at Wheeler Bent.

"I'm pleased with what you've done, Wheeler," he said. "I'm pleased with what you've just said. I was afraid that there might be a mean streak in you . . . and I'm glad that you don't carry any grudges back from Tower Creek. You go inside and get the fire started, will you? It's going to be chilly this evening."

Wheeler Bent went toward the barn house, stepping stiffly, for his spinal column was congealing with happiness.

"Now for me," Eugenia said, lying back in greater comfort against the root of the tree.

"Speak up and tell me," said her father.

"What's the use? You know. You know everything. You always do."

"Do you think I spy on you?" he asked suddenly.

"Great heavens," said the girl. "Of course you don't."

"Thanks, Gene," he said. "But there's always a lot of earthworms and insects buzzing around anxious to curry favor with a rich man by telling him things. You know that I'm a rich man, Gene?"

"Of course I know that."

"You know that I'm very rich?"

"Yes. I know that, too."

"You know that I'm *too* rich?"

She sat up and looked straight at him.

"Well?" she said.

"I'm too rich. And I've only got one child, and I'm sixty years old. Understand?"

She was silent.

"And," he went on, "I care about that one child so much that when a lot of busybody fools come to me whispering, I have to listen to what they say. This time they've said quite a lot. Well, I've never talked to you like this before, and I'll never talk like this again. You can have as free a rein as you want, but I know that you'll think about what it means to me now and then. That's all I'll say."

Chapter Thirteen

What her father had said was so important that the girl had to think it over for a time. She watched the slow motion of the knife as it was drawn through the wood. She saw the curling filament of the shaving that separated from the stick.

Finally she said: "Do you want me to tell you everything?"

"If you think it's wise," he answered. "Remember that I'm a hard man and a stern man, and a man of action, Gene. If I don't like what I hear from you, I'm reasonably sure to try to do something about it. And what I attempt to do may be pretty radical."

She thought that over for a moment, then she said: "Well, no matter what you have to do about it, you must know exactly what's happened. I'm going to tell you."

He went on whittling. His face looked younger than ever, but the eyes were darker and deeper hollows. Increasing years simply made him seem a man who is a trifle ill, or who is convalescing.

She said: "Everything you've heard from the gossips is true, and a lot they haven't heard is true, too. A man walked in on the dance . . . a man the sheriff wanted to keep out of it. He made another fellow introduce him to me, and he sat down and talked. I liked him a lot. The sheriff appeared and ran him through a window. After a while he got Wheeler away from me and knocked him cold, and took his clothes and his mask, and walked in through the door again as though he were Wheeler. He came up and talked to me. I knew it wasn't Wheeler, of course. But I danced with him."

Judge Tyrrel stopped his whittling, folded his knife, put it into a pocket, and slipped his hands around one knee. Braced in this manner, in a poised position, he looked out of the darkness of his brows at the girl and waited for the rest of her story.

She saw that he was moved, and she was frightened, but she went on: "Well, I danced with him. He told me that Wheeler hadn't been hurt. He said that he would call on me today, before night. Before the twilight ended, he would call on me. Here."

She stopped and waited.

After a time the judge said: "The name of him is Jingo, isn't it?"

"Yes."

"What's his real name?"

"I don't know. He says that his real name is only for the girl that marries him."

"Perhaps you're that girl," suggested the judge.

The calmness of his voice increased her fear. Suddenly she regretted the frankness with which she had talked to him, and she remembered many a story she had heard of grim things that he had done in business. People who stood in his way were simply pushed aside. That was always the fashion of the judge.

She thought of the bright and fearless figure of Jingo, and she thought of the calm and resistless strength of her father's mind. If the two ever met in conflict, what would happen? Out of the distance there was a groaning sound as a big load of hay came down the road, the brakes shuddering against the iron tires.

The judge said again: "Perhaps Jingo intends to honor you with his hand, Gene?"

The irony in his voice and words terrified her more than ever.

"Don't you see, Father," she said, "that it's all a joke? He's just a wild, irresponsible, careless fellow."

"The sort of a character that the sheriff of the county doesn't wish to allow into a dance hall," said Tyrrel. "Why did the sheriff want to keep him out?"

"Well, there had been a fight that day. Jingo was in it."

"What sort of a fight?"

"With guns," she admitted. She hated to go on. She could see how her father would judge the thing.

"Where was the fight?" Tyrrel asked.

"In a saloon . . . in Tower Creek." Then she went on rapidly: "The other fellow was cheating at cards. Jingo shot him. *After* the other man had pulled a gun. It was just self-defense."

The judge raised his hand, saying: "When you're older, you'll hear other stories of men who shoot down others in self-defense. Cold-blooded rascals who spend half their time practicing with guns and know that they can depend on their skill. Men against whom an ordinary honest citizen has no chance. No more chance than a pigeon has against a hawk."

"Jingo wouldn't spend half his time practicing at any sort of work," she declared.

The dark brows of her father were turned constantly toward her.

"Afterward," he said, "when he had shot down his man, he wanted more amusement, and it seemed to him a good idea to go to the dance and defy the sheriff and take for his dancing partner my daughter. He tricked the sheriff out of the way once. The next time he got your escort away from you, knocked him senseless, took his clothes, and paraded past the sheriff a second time. And you were willing to dance with the blackguard?"

The words were emphatic enough, but not once was the voice of the judge lifted. She saw how things were going. She wished heartily that she had not made her free confession.

"And then," said the judge, "the brazen scoundrel

has the effrontery to tell you that he intends to call on you before tonight. Is that it?"

"It's just a sort of game with him," the girl tried to explain. "He doesn't mean . . ."

"Eugenia," said the judge, "I want you to be perfectly honest with me. Do you like him very much?"

She wanted to talk down about Jingo, but that appeal to her honesty staggered her.

She said: "I'll tell you frankly . . . I've never met a man I liked so well."

The judge smiled without mirth.

"I've told you that I might have to take strict measures. I'll tell you now what those measures are going to be. You're to confine yourself to the house until dark. And after that we'll see. In the meantime, I can pledge my faith to you that young Mister Jingo will *not* call on you before twilight has ended."

She was on her feet by this time. "What do you mean to do?" she gasped at him.

"I simply mean to keep trespassers off the premises," said the judge. "When you go in, tell the cook to get Hooker and send him to me. Hooker's back, watching the putting away of the hay in the barns."

She wanted to beg her father to limit his anger. She wanted to urge the youth and the careless mind of Jingo. She wanted to say that Jingo was like his name—just a reckless, strange sort of a person. But she saw that every word she spoke on his behalf would serve to increase the calm anger of Judge Tyrrel. So she went back into the house and sent the cook on the errand.

So Lem Hooker came out to meet the big boss. Lem was a fellow tall and very lean, and he had a long and very lean face with prominent buckteeth. The projection of his teeth made Lem seem to smile all day long, and he had spent his life trying to prove that the good nature was only a matter of the surface, and not of the soul. He had a bull terrier's love of trouble, and the men who worked under him on the big ranch knew all about his nature.

When he came up to the judge, he tipped his hat. The only thing in the world that he loved—outside of a fight—was Judge Tyrrel. He would have hanged a good many years ago had it not been for the judge. But there was more than a sense of gratitude in Hooker. He looked up to Tyrrel as one strong man may to another who is still stronger.

The judge said: "If you've heard any gossip from Tower Creek, you've heard about the carryings-on of a fellow called Jingo."

"I have," Lem Hooker said.

"Know what he looks like?"

"Five feet eleven. About a hundred and sixty pounds. Dark eyes and skin. Mighty handsome sort of a gent."

"He says," went on the judge, "that he's going to call on Eugenia before night. Before the end of the twilight, he's going to call on Eugenia, no matter where she may be on the place. Your job is to see that he doesn't arrive. Search the house first. Then search the barns. Give every man on the place a description of the man. Make sure that he's nowhere near us. When you've made sure of that, stretch a cordon around the house and the barns. There's an early moon, but you won't need its light. If he doesn't show up before night, he's missed his bet. Hooker, this may sound to you like a joke, but it's not."

"In this here kind of a game of tag," said Hooker, "somebody's likely to stay down after he's 'it'."

The judge considered for a long moment. He began to whittle at his stick again.

"Lem," he said, "this fellow Jingo is a gunman and gambler and worthless idler, I take it. If he intrudes on these premises, I think I'm right in my own mind . . . I know I'm right in the law . . . if I stop him at any cost. You understand?"

The right hand of Lem Hooker stole in a subtle gesture toward his hip and came slowly away again. A real smile allowed his big buckteeth to flash in the slanting light of the sun.

"I sure understand," he said.

The judge said one thing more, deliberately.

"If Jingo manages to break through, I won't be expecting to have you around tomorrow."

112

Chapter Fourteen

The work of Lem Hooker was always done thoroughly. He got a group of men together first and searched the house from the attic to the floor. Then he went through the barns. He had thirty hands or more hauling hay, leading the derrick horses, handling the big Jackson forks, or stowing the hay away in the tops of the barns. There were plenty of hands present, therefore, and when the search had been completed without finding Jingo, Lem Hooker made a little speech to the gang in which he described Jingo.

"He ain't here now," he said. "All you need to do is to make sure that he don't get here later on. Now go to work . . . and keep your eyes open. Act like he could burrow underground, or turn himself into a load of hay, or drop down out of the sky on a pair of wings. If any of you ain't packing a gun, go and load yourselves down. In this here game, the gent that's tagged is going to know he's 'it' without nobody telling him."

In the meantime, Jingo and the Parson had cut across country, taking their ease on the way, since there was no great hurry in performing the journey. The tireless trot of Lizzie, which would have broken the bones of any man other than the

Parson, continued steadily, and Jingo's fierce-eyed horse easily kept pace.

So they came, in the heat of the afternoon, to the crest of a hill from which they looked down on the white windings of the road that ran through a valley beneath them. The wind was traveling down the valley. Now and then it picked up a whirl of dust and carried it like a ghost over the road. The day was hot. The wind blew the heat even through flannel shirts, and scorched the skin.

The Parson said: "Down yonder, Jingo, there's a thing that looks to me like a dog-gone' oasis, and today's hot enough to be a desert. You see them trees and the red roof in the middle of 'em, and the shed that sticks out onto the side of the road? That's a place where a man could get a glass of beer, I'm thinking."

"And show our faces and show our hands?" said Jingo. "Would that make any sense?"

"I'll throw a coin," the Parson suggested.

Jingo laughed. "All right," he said.

The coin spun, winking high in the air, off the thumb of the Parson.

"Heads," said Jingo.

The half dollar spatted in the great hard palm of the Parson.

"Tails," he said, closing his fingers over it.

"I didn't see it," answered Jingo.

"Hey, you wouldn't argue about a glass of beer, would you?" asked the Parson.

Jingo laughed again.

"You love trouble, Parson," he said. "You're going to have a ten-course dinner of it before very long. You're going to have trouble roasted with the feathers on. But come along."

He turned his horse down the slope, and they swept up in good style to the front of the tavern. It was a comfortable type, white-painted, with watering troughs stretching in front, enough of them to accommodate a sixteen-mule team with the spans still harnessed to their singletrees. A big wooden awning stood out from the front of the saloon, so that buggies and carts and horsemen could come right up to the door of the place and hitch at the inside rack. Above the saloon rose the vast green cloud of the trees.

The Parson and Jingo went inside. The floor was black-spotted with water that had recently been flung over it, and there were fresh strewings of sawdust arranged in dim lines as it had fallen from the fingers, somewhat like iron filings on a paper above a magnet. The air was damp and cool. A windmill was clanking not far from the house, and Jingo could hear the whisper of the gushing water. The sour-sweet pungency of many drinks was in the air. The bar rail had been scarred by ten thousand heels and scratched to brightness, but at that moment Jingo and the Parson were the only people in the place, except for the bartender and a boy who was washing windows.

The bartender looked like an ex–prize fighter. But now his blunt face and his chunky body were layered over with soft fat. He was constantly moist with perspiration. When he picked up a glass, he left his finger marks outlined in mist.

"We'll have a game of seven-up," said the Parson. "Give us some cards, bartender. We'll play a game while we have a drink. Take something with us?"

The bartender admitted that it might be a good idea. He took a small beer that was mostly froth, and punched the register for three full-size drinks. He put out two packs of cards, and as the Parson and Jingo sat down at a corner table to finish their beer slowly and play a hand or two of seven-up, the barman motioned the boy to him from the window that he was washing.

The Parson was dealing, flicking out the cards with expert fingers.

Jingo said to him: "Did that bartender look you in the chin or in the eyes?"

"He slammed me in the eyes once, and after that he couldn't look higher than my stomach," said the Parson. He announced, immediately after-ward, that he was shooting the moon. But he was playing his jack for high, and a queen fitted neatly on top of it out of Jingo's cards.

"There's something on the bartender's mind," urged Jingo. "Did you ever hit him while you were wading through a crowd?"

"I've got a memory for mugs," the Parson answered, "and I never saw his map before."

A door slammed with a jangling of a wire screen at the rear of the place. The boy was gone from the saloon, and the bartender was polishing the bar.

The Parson added: "What's eating you, Jingo?"

"He's sent the kid out on an errand, and the errand is about us," said Jingo. "He's thinking so hard about us right now that he's turning redder than his work oughta make him."

"Well?" asked the Parson.

"We've got to make him call the boy back," Jingo advised.

"Got to?"

"Yes."

"Hey, bartender, what's your name?" the Parson demanded loudly.

"Wilson," came the answer from the saloon-keeper as he continued to polish off the bar.

"Wilson," said the Parson, "I wanna take a look at that boy. Call him back."

Wilson continued his work. He lifted his eyes for one brief glance at the giant, and dropped them again to his cloth.

Then he said: "The kid's busy."

"Maybe he's too busy to suit us," said the Parson.

Wilson tossed his cloth aside, leaned, and picked up something from the shelf under the bar. He looked not at his two guests, but straight ahead. It was perfectly plain that he had taken up a gun.

The Parson laid one pack of cards on top of the other and tapped them into a trim-edged little mass.

"I ain't a mind-reader," he said, "but sometimes I can tell a fool when he's in the middle of a play."

He took the two packs between his hands with a reversing grip, and slowly, without a jerk, twisted the stiff mass in two. He flung the mass from him, and they fell with a little rattling shower on the floor.

"Now call back that kid!" the Parson barked.

The bartender stared for an instant at the torn packs that were scattered before him. Then he turned toward the door behind the bar.

"Don't leave the room!" the Parson snapped with authority.

Wilson stood fast. His back was turned to them. He was breathing so hard that his head kept lifting and nodding a little.

Finally he went to an open window and sent out a long, shrilling whistle. After that he returned to the bar and began to rub the wood meditatively with the heel of his hand, looking with vague eyes straight before him.

"Maybe he's calling up all hell to drop in and visit us," muttered the Parson to Jingo.

Jingo sat back from the table a little, at ease.

"Maybe," he said. "I thought we'd get more trouble than beer down here."

Presently the rear door opened with a squeak and closed with a jingling rattle again. The bare-footed boy came into the saloon. He had a tattered straw hat on his head now. His eyes were big and pale with excitement.

"Go on with that window. Forget the other thing," said Wilson.

The boy gaped. Then, without a word, went back toward the window.

"Bring over some more beer," the Parson said. "Bring one for yourself and sit down."

There was the same hesitation in the manner of Wilson, but finally he obeyed. He put down two glasses before them.

"Where's your own?" asked the Parson.

Wilson shook his head.

"Now, then," went on the Parson, "I wanna know where you was sending that kid. Talk soft. No reason why he should hear you."

"I was sending him to town," Wilson answered.

"Why?"

"I got a lot of curiosity," the Parson explained. "What was he going to do in town?"

"Get some nails," said Wilson. He looked straight at the Parson.

"Nails for what?" asked the Parson.

"Nails to use in the making of some chicken coops. They use up a lot of nails."

"What would you want chicken coops for?" asked the Parson. "Ain't the range free for chickens to walk on?"

"Yeah, and for coyotes to eat them," Wilson replied. "Besides, they're always scratching up my vegetable garden."

"Let's take a look at the vegetable garden," suggested Jingo.

Wilson said nothing, but led the way out through the back of the house, across the floor of a very clean kitchen, and down the back steps into a fenced yard irrigated from the windmill. There was a growing crop of alfalfa that covered half the ground. The rest was given over to vegetables. Off to the side were a series of chicken runs enclosed in bright new wire. And in one of the runs there were no chickens, only a quantity of slats, strips of one-by-two boards, and several coops already completed.

Jingo went to the coops.

"It's all right, by thunder," said the Parson. "There's the coops he's making, sure enough."

"It can't be right," Jingo said calmly.

He looked about him. On a workbench that was improvised out of a pair of sawbucks and some cross boards lay a hammer and a saw. There was not a nail in sight. Still he searched, and at last lifted a small fold of tarpaulin that lay on the ground under the bench. Inside it were a couple of pounds of glittering new nails.

Jingo came back and confronted the pale, set face of Wilson.

"Now come out with it," said Jingo.

Wilson made no answer. He kept looking vacantly.

"Persuade him, Parson," said Jingo.

The Parson laid his enormous hand upon the fat, soft shoulder of the bartender.

"Talking is the best way," said the Parson.

"Aw," muttered Wilson suddenly, "they want your scalps, is all. I was to tip them off if you came this way."

"Who were you to tip off?" asked Jingo.

"Jake Rankin and the other two."

"What other two?"

"Boyd and Oliver."

"What do Boyd and Oliver look like?"

"Boyd's a little runt with a face like a rat. Oliver's a bulldog. He's gotta pull in his jaw to make his teeth meet."

"Where are they now?" asked Jingo.

"I've double-crossed them and I've double-crossed you," Wilson said sullenly. "Now I'm through double-crossing. You don't get any more talk out of me."

"Don't we?" the Parson said, his vast hands twitching. "I dunno but what I could get something out of you."

"Let him alone," Jingo commanded. "He's not going to keep walking crooked. And as long as he

121

goes straight, we leave him alone. Wilson, I'm glad we found out that Jake Rankin and another pair are on the look-out. Boyd and Oliver . . . are they pretty tough?"

"They ain't pretty, but they're tough," Wilson informed him. "You gents watch your step, I'd say. Get out of this neck of the woods, if you got any sense."

"Why," Jingo announced, smiling, "I never refuse to go to a dance so long as I know who I've got to dance with. Come along, Parson. We're losing time."

Chapter Fifteen

Travel up the well-graded road to Blue Water was obviously too dangerous a business, so long as Rankin and two others were watching the way at some point. Parson and Jingo cut back through the hills, and so arrived, in the late afternoon, within view of the ranch of Judge Tyrrel. They left their horses behind the crest of a hill and sat down in a clump of brush that screened them, while it allowed them to look intimately down on the buildings and the men who were working at the barns.

"Pretty, ain't it?" asked the Parson. "Look at the way the evening is starting ahead of time over yonder in the ravine. Look at the way the snow is shining down at us. Look at the mob of those fellows handling the hay into the barns. Pretty, I'd say it is."

At the end of each of the three great barns there was a wagon of hay being unloaded by the use of a great four-tined Jackson fork that was lifted by a team of two horses, led or driven. They could hear the slow groaning of the pulleys as the horses started the forkful up. They could hear the click and then the smooth rumbling as the load ran back along the iron running rail at the top of a barn, while the tugging team of derrick horses no longer strained at their collars, but walked easily forward, their traces slack.

The observers were so close that they could even hear, dim and far away, the voice of the headman who stowed the hay, calling—"Dump!"—when the loaded fork had reached the desired spot.

"How'd you like to be in there, Parson?" asked Jingo. "There's the place for a fellow like you. You'd be worth a whole crew of three or four in there. You could shift a whole load with your pitchfork, and every time you put down your foot on the loose stuff, it would be worth the drop of a beater in a baling machine. You'd be worth your weight . . . in lead."

The Parson grinned.

"The time was," he said, "when I figured that it was a proud and noble dog-gone' thing to be able to heave twice as much on a pitchfork as anybody else could. I used to roll bales on a Little Giant press, and throw up the bales four high, and sometimes I'd chuck up a few five high. The ranchers, they used to like to have me working on the hay baler, because they could roll off the top two tiers of the stack onto their wagons afterward without no derrick at all. But after a while I figured out that a strong head was better than a strong back. I've given up working like that, Jingo."

"What do you do now?" Jingo asked curiously.

"I hunt for hard-shelled crabs and crack 'em,

and eat the white meat," said the Parson, moving his hands as though he were breaking a crab in two like a piece of bread.

"That sort of business is hard on the hands," Jingo advised, grinning.

"Yeah," agreed the Parson, "but now I'm resting up. All I gotta do is follow the lion and get fat on what he leaves of his kill."

He chuckled as he said this, and Jingo, eying him almost tenderly, remarked: "Someday we're going to have it out, Parson."

"It'll make a lot of dust," said the Parson. "But I'll have to break you up small enough for pocket size one of these days. You're too fresh, Jingo."

Jingo smiled meditatively. He waved toward the picture before them.

"The whole world knows that we're coming here," he observed.

"The whole world knows that you're coming . . . and that I'm with you," corrected the Parson. "It wouldn't be enough for you to bust in on that dance, you had to stand up and announce that you're going to call on the lady at her own home. Well, go on and call, and meet your finish. Because that's what it will be when you try to get into that house. I'll call for the body tomorrow."

He rolled a cigarette. Jingo took it out of his hand and threw it away.

"If we're close enough to see the dust come out of every forkful of that hay," said Jingo, "they're close enough to see the smoke come out of this patch of brush. We might as well be careful."

"All right," said the Parson. "Tell me what scheme you've got in your crazy head?"

"I haven't any scheme," Jingo answered.

"Hey!" cried the Parson. "You mean that you've rode out here all the way without no idea in your head of how you're going to get into that house?"

"Never worry about a bridge till you come to it," answered Jingo. "They've got more men about than I figured on. That's the chief trouble. And a fellow like Judge Tyrrel is apt to be thorough-minded. It might just happen that he won't *want* me to call on his girl."

"Maybe he won't know that you're going to come?" the Parson suggested hopefully.

"A fellow like Tyrrel knows everything," said Jingo. "Besides, she'll tell him. A girl like that doesn't keep secrets from the head of the family. That's the difference, Parson, between her and the rest. That's why she has clean eyes. Because she washes her mind clean every day of her life. Little secrets are what dirty up the souls of most women. But there's nothing small about her."

"She's the queen, eh?" the Parson said.

"That's what she is."

"Then a rosy chance you've got of getting her for yourself," said the Parson.

"I keep running," Jingo answered, "not because I expect to win the race, but because I like the

126

exercise. But how am I to get into that house?"

"My head," the Parson admitted, "is as empty as a dog-gone' bell. There ain't any way you can get into the house."

"Suppose that I were to sneak into one of the barns?" suggested Jingo. "And . . . Look here, Parson. Do you think that Tyrrel's men will be wearing guns on account of you and me?"

"On account of you, they certain sure will be wearing guns," replied the Parson. "And when they salt you down with lead, you'll stay dead as long as a side of pork."

"Simply because a fellow is coming to call?" Jingo commented. "It's absurd for them to go that far."

"Well, suppose that the girl has a kind of a notion that you're the prince of the range, and her father knows what she feels? Ain't he going to do what he can to side-step you? And if you come around there trespassing . . . mightn't you be a burglar or something? But hurry up with your ideas. It's going to be sundown before very long."

Beneath them, two more hay wagons came groaning around the side of the hill, running down the grade against the brakes, the horses backing into their breechings and shuffling their hoofs, while the long poles thrust out and up, swaggering from side to side.

"Well," said Jingo, "there's only one thing for me to do, and that's to turn myself into hay. Once

I get into those barns, I'm a poor fool if I can't wangle it as far as the house."

"Turn yourself into hay?" Parson said. "Now, whatcha mean by that?"

"Keep the horses and stay near this spot," answered Jingo. "I've got an idea that may bring me nothing but the tines of a Jackson fork among my ribs, but I'm going to try it out."

"Well, go to it," said the Parson.

He held out his vast hand and took that of Jingo with an almost gentle pressure.

"If anything happens to you," the Parson said, "I'm going to take and kick Judge Tyrrel and his whole ranch into a stack of kindling wood."

"Thanks," said Jingo. "But nothing is going to happen. I've got luck in my bones."

With that he left the brush, ran back down the rear slope of the hill, and came out through a little gullet just as the last of the two wagons was passing.

The Parson, from his post of vantage, could see his companion climb up the back of the hayrack and wriggle instantly, with snake-like speed, into the top of the load. And, lifting his big hands, the Parson shook them in a silent wonder at the sky.

Jingo had tied his bandanna over his face up to his eyes. He would have been glad to cover the eyes, also, for the dust and chaff that stirred in the load of hay threatened to blind him. Breathing through the silk, he was at least assured of not stifling.

He kept working until he was at what he felt to the right depth in the upper layer of the hay. His hope was simply that he would be included in a forkful of the hay, and that when the Jackson fork was dumped in the mow, he would fall with it, and be able to wriggle through the dust cloud and the flying hay out of the observation of the men who were in the mow.

He felt that he had one chance in five, but he was accustomed to taking the short end of long odds. The chances against him were that he would be found as soon as the driver of the load began to walk over it after halting his wagon beside the barn; that the Jackson fork itself would be fleshed in his body; that even if that were not the case, the weight of his body would prove that something was wrong when the forkful was lifted by the derrick team, and that, if the fall from the traveling beam at the top of the barn were very great, he might be stunned or even break his neck when the fork was tripped. Last of all, of course, there was the very high chance that the men in the barn, stowing the hay, would discover him as he tried to wriggle into hiding.

When he added up these chances, he told himself that he was the greatest fool in the world. He was prepared to slide out from the load, but at that moment he heard many voices all about him, and over the amber sunshine that seeped through the hay above his face there passed a cool wall of shadow. The wagon halted, and he knew that he was under the door of the barn.

Whatever he feared, it was too late to make a change now. He had to submit.

Fear in a vast wave came over him, stifling him. After all, the thing had not gone very far. It was only a jest, a prank, and if he appeared out of the load of hay, he would be thrown off the place, to be sure, but he would be thrown off with no more than jeers and laughter.

But pride was the controlling devil in the heart of Jingo. And when he thought of being hustled off the ranch, he set his teeth grimly and waited.

And still the fear was choking him. He heard the rustling and crunching of the hay as the driver of the wagon, leaving his seat, caught the guide rope of the big Jackson fork with its array of four glistening steel tines, each sharper than a dagger. Those curving teeth would run through his body as through butter. And the driver was coming aft on the load to commence forking it off from that end where Jingo lay!

Chapter Sixteen

Before the unloading commenced, however, there was an argument that made Jingo fear that he had made this journey for nothing, perhaps. And that he would have to lie there in the load of hay, able only to sneak away for safety during the middle of the night.

A man's voice nearby said: "It's damned near sunset time. There ain't enough time to snake off this load. It'll be getting dark up there in the mow. We ought to quit right here."

"What's the good?" said the gruff voice of the driver. "We gotta work all night, don't we? What's the good of knocking off this job and starting to walk a beat? Is that any good? You're going to be tired of that before morning, I can tell you."

"It's a fool's game, anyway," said the other. "He ain't going to come anywhere near."

"Sure he ain't, but we'll get extra pay for the time we put in walking around. And suppose he *does* show up, the gent that pots him will get a cash present that'll keep him flush for a year."

"He won't show up. Not even Jingo is fool enough to try to walk in through the whole gang, all for the sake of a joke, too."

"Well, sink your fork, and we'll get that load off."

Jingo dared not stir for fear of making a noise that might betray him, but he shrank inwardly and lay still in dread. He had a more desperate impulse than ever to spring up from the hay and get out of this pinch. For it was clear that everything he feared might happen was actually in the air. The big gangs of men who worked for Judge Tyrrel were armed and expected to remain on duty all through the night to prevent the approach of Jingo.

And now he lay like a fool in a load of hay, waiting to be pronged like a senseless beast.

He heard the rope run with a loose rattle in the pulley far overhead. Then there was a great crash in the hay near him, a puffing of dust and chaff into his face.

"All-l-l right!" yelled the wagoner.

The derrick driver called to his team and snapped his black snake. The pulley above the wagon rattled again, then groaned as the rope began to straighten at the weight of the embedded fork. The whole load of hay shuddered. There was a pulling on the masses in which Jingo lay so that he hoped that his own body would be drawn up at this first venture. There with a tearing, crunching sound the fork-load was torn clear of the rest of the hay. The rope ran up more easily, more swiftly. High above, the fork clinked as it struck the carrier and the iron wheels of the carrier rumbled softly as the load was swept along that hanging track into the mow.

"Dump!" called a stifled voice inside.

There was a rushing sound followed by the thump of a good, solid blow.

Jingo closed his eyes and shut back a groan. It seemed that the mow of this barn was just beginning to fill, and there might be a fall of forty feet from the roof to the low level of the mowed hay.

"Don't try to snake off the whole load in two bites!" yelled the angry voice of the derrick driver. "What you trying to do? Break the backs of these horses?"

"You going to teach me how to handle a Jackson fork?" the driver asked sternly.

"Yeah, and I could do it!" cried the derrick man. "Any ten-year-old kid could teach you things about handling a Jackson fork."

"Aw, shut up, Pete," called one from a distance.

"I ain't going to shut up. He's trying to stick my team here. He's trying to fetch off this whole load in two bites."

There was a sudden down-rushing of a force above Jingo. A weight fell on him.

A knife thrust of pain drove into his right leg. He jerked the leg away from the tine that had hooked it. It was hard to move. It was almost hard to breathe, the hay all about him was so wedged and bound together in a mass.

He thrust a hand upward, forcing it slowly through the most compacted part of the hay until his fingers reached the cold of steel. He closed his grip well up on one tine. In that way, he could hope to keep himself from spilling out of the forkful—if only the horses were able to lift him with the rest of the burden.

"All-l-l right!" yelled the wagoner.

The rope drew up its slack with a jerk. Jingo was wrenched up a yard or so. Then he was dropped again.

The dust forced its way through the bandanna and almost choked him. He was half-blinded, too, and barely made out the distant voice of the derrick driver.

"What you got on that fork? You trying to kill my team?"

The wagoner responded with a roar: "Throw the leather into them cayuses! You try to tell me again how to handle a Jackson fork, and I'll get down and give you a bust on the nose. Go on!"

"I'm going to talk to you later!" shouted the furious derrick man. "Get up, boys!"

The whip cracked. Jingo was jerked upward again. With a great tearing noise in his ears, the fork-load that included him tore loose.

The load swung in and bumped the side of the barn.

Slowly it began to mount, with a great groaning of the ropes and the pulleys.

"What's in that forkful?" shouted a distant voice.

Up went Jingo, with a dizziness growing in his

head, his grip slipping a little on the polished round of the tine he was grasping. With a bump and a click, the fork jumped into the carrier. The load slid forward. A wave of hotter air bathed Jingo. He seemed to be hurling forward at great speed.

"Dump!" yelled a voice from beneath.

The tine wrenched out of his fingers. He dropped, making himself loose and limp from head to foot.

There was a stunning shock. His knees drove up and rapped against his chin.

Out of the dimness of his mind he heard a man exclaiming: "There was a rock or something in that forkful."

"Naw. The hay gets wadded sometimes," said another. "You take where there's some green, and it gets all wadded up hard. That's all."

Sounds of angry wrangling came from outside the barn as Jingo, hearing the footfalls come crunching toward him, tried to wriggle away through the loose masses.

He heard the hiss of pitchfork tines thrust in not far from his head. A mass of hay was flopped down on top of him. Someone was trampling him down, with stamping feet, beating his body, choking him.

Then the footfalls withdrew in the noisy brittleness of the hay.

Jingo lay still. He felt he was stifling. But he

swore to himself that there *must* be air enough percolating through the porous mass. He had only to keep himself in hand and prevent hysteria from grasping him by the throat.

The heat baked him. The chaff itched his skin. The wound in his leg ached and burned.

"Hey!" yelled someone. "There's blood in this here!"

"Yeah. Somebody pitchforked a field mouse, maybe. I seen that happen," said another.

The field mouse lay very still, finding it easier to breathe because he wanted to laugh.

Another forkful ran along the carrier with a distant rumbling sound, and then dropped, but not near him. As the men in the barn began to mow away the fresh hay, trampling noisily, Jingo started to wriggle up to the surface, only moving when he heard other sounds.

So he came like a swimmer to such a position that his face was above the level of the hay and at last he could breathe. It was sunset time. Through the great open door of the mow to the west the red light poured and filled the dusty air inside with clouds of smoke and of dim fire. The forms of the men in the mow, as they worked, seemed larger than human. The tines of their pitchforks flashed like thin lights. They were cursing the heat, the length of the day. This sort of thing was a dog's work and a dog's life, they said.

Meanwhile the Jackson fork was regularly

bringing in fresh loads until the voice of the man on the wagon outside called, thin and far away: "Here's the last bit, boys!"

It came up with a rush, as though the derrick team were trotting. The fork crashed against the carrier above. The load of hay entered like an armful of flame, swept back into dimness, streamed down when the fork was dumped, like water from a height. The great Jackson fork hung gleaming from the iron runway, swaying back and forth like a great four-toothed jaw opening and closing.

And Jingo had been in the grasp of those teeth!

The men from the mow climbed out and down. The loudness of their voices no longer rolled through the barn as through a cavern. The wagon outside went off on rumbling wheels. Two men were disputing savagely not far away. And Jingo was left to the heat of the haymow, where small rustling sounds and crinkling had already commenced in the hay.

Chapter Seventeen

On a joining of the second-story tie beams, which offered a little platform perhaps two feet square, Jingo made his hasty toilet. It took time, and he had little time to spare. But he could not appear for his call covered with dust and his clothes full of wisps of hay. And there was the matter of his wounded leg, for another thing.

He undressed, tore up his undershirt, and made a bandage. The wound had closed its small mouth, and only a trickle of blood was coming from it after the first gush. There was a big, dark, wet spot of it on the inside of his trousers leg. But since he was to make his call just at twilight, he would have to hope that it would not be seen as a discoloration.

He picked the bits of hay out of his clothes and shook the dust from them before he dressed again.

One part of his way was clear before him. High above, there was a trap door in the roof, and to this he mounted, climbing up a ladder. He looked from the door into the smoking red of the dying sunset. He looked down toward the ground and saw men already walking back and forth. A long, loose line of them extended as far as he could see around the barns and the house, which was the building next to him. He saw the glimmer of the barrels of rifles and shotguns. They would be on the alert now, as the right season of the day approached for Jingo's well-advertised attempt to call on Judge Tyrrel's daughter.

The distinguishing feature of the roof of the barn that Judge Tyrrel had decided to use for a house was a little roof garden or captain's walk that had been built out around the trap door such as that through which Jingo was looking. And Tyrrel had set off the high platform with a flagstaff from which a big silk American flag bloomed and faded as the wind extended it or let it shrink from the sunset light.

Jingo saw his chance. There was no way of getting to the house of the judge by walking on the ground—not under the eyes of all the men who were surrounding the place. Already they were bringing out lanterns, encircling the house with a cordon of light.

But there was another possibility of entering the place.

Jingo went back inside the barn and worked his way to the runway of the Jackson fork, and then cut a great length of the derrick rope. This he coiled around his shoulder. With that weight, he returned to his trap door in the roof. He made a running knot, shook out a noose, then pushed the trap door wide open and stepped out on the slant of the roof.

It was not easy. The roof slanted so that it made

it hard for him to stand and also constricted the area in which he could swing his noose. Above all, he stood up there on the roof with the dull light of the horizon encircling him—and below, pacing the ground, there were expert marksmen looking for just such a target.

However, he widened his noose, swung it until it was hissing in the air about his head, then threw it with all the strength of his arm.

He threw it with so much strength, in fact, that the impetus jerked him off his feet. He fell flat, skidding down over the shakes that covered the roof. Only at the rain gutter, his fingers got a grip and saved him from diving headlong to the ground.

He looked up and saw that his noose had fallen fair and true over the flagstaff of Judge Tyrrel. It seemed to him that he had put out a long, thin arm on the judge.

Then he heard, from beneath, voices talking.

"What's that rope doing?" asked one.

"I never seen it before."

"I'll go up and take a look."

"There ain't any light in the barn to climb by. You'll break your neck."

"I'll get Tom Farrell, then. Farrell will know if that rope had oughta be there."

"Yeah, you go that way, and I'll go this, and we'll get Tom Farrell."

Jingo was already crawling back up the sharp

slope of the roof. He pulled the length of derrick rope taut and fastened it to a beam inside the trap door. After that he walked down the roof and began to swing himself hand over hand along the rope.

It swayed up and down, it vibrated under his hands, as though it were endowed with a snaky life and with an urgent desire to shake him from his grasp. The rope was worn. The frayed strands bristled like a steel cable and cut the palms of his hands. And every moment he waited to hear from beneath the outcry that would announce that he was discovered.

Then his feet no longer dangled over nothingness. They struck the slant of the opposite roof. A moment later, he was on the captain's walk of Judge Tyrrel's house. And, right before him, an open door offered a way into the place.

He crouched for a moment, breathing hard. He had come a good distance, to be sure, but he was by no means safe; he was by no means at the end of his journey, and the day was darkening fast. He looked up, and could see a fine golden point of light in the sky. Arcturus was already beginning to shine.

Well, there was still plenty of green light banding the horizon, and it must be called dusk until the full battery of the stars had begun to shine.

Where would the girl be?

Alone in her room perhaps, or else in the midst of many others.

He entered the darkness and the warm air inside the house. There was a long flight of steps that turned into a hall. The hall ended at a door. He opened it and stepped out on a narrow balcony that overlooked the huge central hall of the judge's house. There were little round circles of lamplight, here and there. A long table was being set. And as the chill of the evening commenced, a great fire had been lit on a hearth of such dimensions as Jingo never had seen before in all his life.

He saw the judge seated beside the fire and was surprised by the shabbiness of his clothes, but he recognized the face that had appeared so often in newspaper photographs. He knew the great spacious brow and the thoughtful inclination of the head.

Then he saw young Wheeler Bent talking with the girl, who sat with her back to the biggest pillar in the room, the huge central support that upheld the middle of the roof and for which a great tree had been felled and squared. It was, in fact, like the mast of a ship.

How could the girl have been placed in a position more difficult for him to reach? Or should he content himself with simply calling to her from the balcony where he then stood?

No, what was in his mind was suddenly to appear before her, while the twilight was still in the sky, and offer his greeting in the most casual manner.

His time was short, not only because the day was dying rapidly, but also because that fellow Tom Farrell might even at this moment be staring up from the ground toward the mysterious rope that extended still from the opposite barn to the house of the judge. Should he have cut that rope away from the flagpole? Well, in that case it would have been found dangling along the side of the barn, to cause even more suspicion than before.

He looked desperately about the hall. He could get out on the big beams. He could descend from one story of them to the other, and if he were sufficiently silent, he might accomplish most of his journey without attracting attention. But how was he to descend the final stage from the lowest beams to the floor?

His wandering eye settled on the only note of color in the entire room—a pair of great, striped curtains that soared upward across the windows that faced the entrance door. It looked like an Indian pattern. It even looked like Indian blanket stuff.

In that case it could be used perhaps.

He was at work in an instant, his boots off and tied about his neck, while he stole like a huge, prowling cat out along the comfortable bulk of the first beam beneath the balcony.

He got out to the center of the room, slid down

an upright to the beams beneath, and crossed the next huge beam until he found himself right at the head of the big curtains.

By the wavering firelight, he could see the strength of the big iron rings that fastened the curtains to their pole. He gripped the cloth and found the fabric of heavy wool.

Well, perhaps he had found the ladder that would take him almost the rest of the way.

The judge was saying: "Cheer up, Eugenia. It's drafty over there. Come here by the fire or you'll be catching cold."

"I'll stay where I am," she answered. "I can look out through the doors, from here, and see the end of the day."

"It's ended now," said the judge, "and your friend Jingo is not going to appear. Eh, Wheeler?"

Wheeler Bent laughed.

"He's a wild rascal, but of course he's not an absolute fool," said Wheeler Bent. "The night has started now."

"Look again, Wheeler," said the girl. "You can still see green in the sky. That isn't in the color of the night sky, is it?"

"Well, grant him five minutes more," Wheeler Bent said.

"I'm glad he hasn't come," said the girl. "If he had come . . . if one of those men had dared to shoot at him . . . Father, will you answer me one thing?"

"Perhaps," said Tyrrel.

"You've put those men on guard only as bluff, of course. They wouldn't dare to shoot, would they?"

"I won't answer that," Tyrrel said. "I want no trespassers on this place and no young ruffians walking into it."

The girl had started up from her chair. Jingo, letting himself down from the beam, got inside one half of the curtain and, gripping the big, stiff folds of it, began to lower himself. It was hard work. The cloth, coarse as canvas, was plenty strong enough to support him, but his weight kept pulling the stuff away from the strongest grip he could fasten on the folds.

He heard the girl crying out: "Father, I'm going out there now and tell them not to shoot. Great heavens, don't you see what that wild man will do? He'll wait till the last minute of the twilight, and then he'll make a dash for the house."

"In that case," the grim voice of Tyrrel said, "it will be about the last dash that he makes at anything. Those men out there will blow him to bits."

"Nonsense, Gene," Wheeler Bent said. "Are you trying to make a hero out of your cowboy tramp? He has too much sense. He won't try to run such a gantlet even to get a smile from you, my dear."

She cried to them again: "None of you understands! He said he would be here, and he'll come. If you had the whole army waiting for him with guns, he would come, nevertheless. Father, you've got to go out now . . . now . . . and tell your men to drop their guns, if he comes . . . because he *must* be on the way this instant."

The judge was sufficiently moved to stand up by the hearth. And Jingo now stood on the floor inside the curtains. The red firelight shook in great tangible waves through the room and set it wavering like images in deep water. Over the dishes and the glasses that had been set out on the long table the light ran like gilding. The glass seemed to burn.

Jingo pulled on his boots and stepped quietly out from his hiding place, walking toward the central pillar so that the light from the hearth would still be divided to either side away from him. In a shuddering, narrow ravine of darkness he stealthily stepped toward the pillar.

The judge answered his daughter: "When a man puts his will against my will, Eugenia, he has to take the chances that luck give him . . . and the troubles that I can put in his way. If your friend Jingo, or Jingle, or whatever his name may be, manages to get to this house, I'll welcome him with an open hand . . . for this evening at least. But if my men can stop him on the way, they're going to blow him to bits as a trespasser. The law supports them. A man's house can be kept sacred from intrusion."

A big fellow, with bells chiming on his spurs,

came striding suddenly through the open doorway.

"Judge Tyrrel," he said, "we gotta go up and have a look at the roof. There's a rope running from the next barn over to your house."

"The devil there is!" the judge cried. "Who put it there?"

"I did," Jingo said, stepping out from the pillar at the side of the girl. "Good evening, Gene. I think I'm just on time?"

Chapter Eighteen

It was like the sudden striking of a blow after the sparring has continued a long time. A quick tension jerked every head. And Jingo watched all of these results from the corner of his eye while he considered the girl, first of all. The shock of his appearance made her rigid for an instant. Then her head tilted back a little, and she began to laugh. She held out her hand, and he took it gravely.

Wheeler Bent got hold of the back of a chair and supported himself. The big fellow by the door was gibbering something.

And then Judge Tyrrel came slowly across the room, saying: "You're Jingo, I suppose? We've been expecting you. But did you rise up out of the floor or just materialize out of the empty air?"

He was not laughing. A smile twisted a bit at his lips, that was all. But he shook hands with Jingo.

The unexpected guest was answering: "I just dropped down into your place, but I landed in the next barn, and not in your house. So I put a rope bridge across and came over that way. I hate crowds, and there were a lot of people walking around on the ground below."

The judge chuckled. After that first long,

straight look, he did not examine Jingo with so much criticism in his eyes. Suddenly he seemed to accept the intruder.

"You'll have supper with us," he said. "Eugenia, see that another place is laid. I think you've met Wheeler Bent before?"

Wheeler Bent had managed to steady himself a little. He made no effort to approach but acknowledged the introduction from a distance. He was white about the lips as though the effort of smiling had numbed his face.

"Oh, yes," he said. "We've met before." He began to frown a little and kept narrowing his eyes.

Jingo understood. He was looking to Wheeler Bent rather smaller than that gentleman's expectation.

"A rope bridge from the next barn," the judge was saying. "And you flew down to the barn with a pair of wings or you rose out of the ground, Jingo?"

"I'd like to tell you," said Jingo. "It's really very simple. But magicians are bound to one another not to tell how they do their little tricks."

"Little tricks?" exclaimed Wheeler Bent. "A man could easily rob a bank with a trick no better than this."

The big cowpuncher who had come through the doorway to announce the discovery of the rope between barn and house had remained motionless all this time. There was only a slight twitching of his body, from time to time, as new ideas struck him like bullets.

Now he said—"Well, dog-gone my hide."—and turned on his heel and departed with his glance trailing over his shoulders toward Jingo. It was plain that Tom Farrell was not satisfied with life or the world, this evening. Perhaps the judge would have something to say, later on, about the efficiency with which his place had been guarded against intrusion.

The girl had gone off to give directions about the alteration in seating at the table.

Wheeler Bent moved like a stunned man toward the open door, from which he stared at the sky that was still faintly stained near the horizon with the twilight green.

And the judge took Jingo nearer to the fire.

"Now, young man," said Judge Tyrrel, "I'd like to hear from you."

Jingo looked into the dark hollows under the great brow of Tyrrel and saw the steady glimmering of the eyes.

"Do you want to know why I came?" he asked.

"I want to know anything you care to tell me about yourself," answered Tyrrel. "Including your name."

"My name," said Jingo, "comes from the African . . ."

"Oh," said the judge, "my girl has told me

already about J. I. Ngo. I thought you might have another name, by this time."

"I hate to throw away gifts," said the young man, "and Jingo is a name that was given to me. If you want to know why I came . . . it's simply because I told your daughter that I'd call on her. But as for the name . . . why, when you travel, you don't take your whole wardrobe with you, I suppose? And Jingo is a good, light traveling name."

The judge smiled his faint smile again.

"Please go on," he said. "You came partly because you wanted to see my daughter and partly because it would be a hard thing to do."

"It's better to do things at a stroke, I always think," answered Jingo. "I'd rather ride than walk. And think of all the walking I'd have to do to get a proper introduction to Judge Tyrrel. However, by just sending word that I'm coming, in this way, the whole place is organized to meet me. Every cowpuncher on the ranch, since he heard that I was coming, has been polishing up . . . his guns. And even Judge Tyrrel is kind enough to pay attention to me. I'd have to be worth two or three millions, at least, to get this much attention from you in any other way."

"Jingo," said Tyrrel, "how long do you intend to ride horses through life?"

"I hope," Jingo said, "that I'll always be in the saddle."

"And work?" asked the judge.

"No work," replied Jingo. "I agree with you about that. I hate work almost as much as you do, Judge Tyrrel."

"Hate it as much as I do? Do I hate work?" repeated the judge, half offended and half curious. "My dear young friend, how much time do you think I have to myself?"

"Nearly every minute," Jingo responded. "You've been daydreaming all your life, I suppose. You have the dream, and then you step into it. So do I. That's where we're different from most people."

"And similar to one another?" Tyrrel asked, his air more watchful than ever.

"Well," Jingo said, "you've kept yourself young, having a good time. I'm doing the same. My good times have horses and guns and poker games in them. Your good times have other things, like cutting down forests and spilling the logs into rivers and sending the big trees through sawmills to make shingles of 'em. You go into a directors' meeting, and I go into a saloon, and the people look on us in about the same way. I break up a meeting, now and then, and so do you. We both look for excitement. You get yours out of raising beef. I get mine out of shooting venison."

"From that angle," Tyrrel said ironically, "we're very much alike."

"I think so," Jingo agreed, laughing easily.

"In that case," said the judge, "we ought to make a combination."

"That's what I think," said Jingo. "That's why I came here."

"If we combine resources," said the judge, his mouth twitching to the side, "what has each of us to offer?"

"Money, of course, doesn't count," Jingo said. "Anyone can make enough of that."

"What *does* count?" asked the judge.

"Reputation," Jingo answered. "You have reputation and a daughter. I have a reputation and need a wife. You can draw the easy deduction, from that."

"There are different kinds of reputation," the judge said.

"Yes," said Jingo, "I was afraid that you'd bring that up."

"And you've known my daughter for about twenty-four hours?" suggested the judge.

"I've spent years planning her," Jingo assured him. "You ought to take that into consideration."

"Young man," said the judge, "I don't know why I'm not more offended."

"Well," said Jingo, "I counted on a sense of humor, sir."

Eugenia came up to them, and the judge said to her with a sudden and almost brutal brusqueness: "Gene, this is a romantic evening. I'd like to know

153

how dizzy you are about Jingo at this moment. Say it out loud."

There was more than the glow of the fire in her face.

"I am a little dizzy," she said.

"Very well," said the judge. "You two sit down and have your talk. Whatever you decide on, now or in the future, I'm not the sort of an old fool who'd disinherit you because of your choices in life. Wheeler, we'll go watch the stars come out."

He turned abruptly away from the two and, picking up a reluctant Wheeler Bent on the way, moved out through the open door and disappeared.

The girl sat by the fire with her chin in her hand and watched the leap and fall of the flames.

Jingo stood opposite her. "My head is full of things I want to say to you," he said. "They've been running in my brain like wild horses."

"Well," said the girl, "you have a right to talk . . . tonight."

"Your father has caught all the wild horses and haltered 'em and put 'em on a lead," said Jingo. "I can't say a word to you now."

"What has he done?" she asked.

"Put me on my silly sense of honor," said Jingo.

She looked up at him suddenly.

"Have you come all this way to be tongue-tied?" she said. "Aren't you going to tell me how you managed to get here, even?"

154

"I was just delivered in a load of hay," Jingo said.

She began to laugh, more with her eyes than her voice. After all, a great many important things can be said without using the tongue.

Chapter Nineteen

As Wheeler Bent and the judge went through the doorway, the judge was saying: "Now, Wheeler, I'm growing old and perhaps pretty much of a fogy. I'd like to know what a young man . . . a man of his own generation . . . frankly thinks about a fellow like Jingo."

Wheeler Bent hastily caressed his little golden mustache. He was so pleased by this invitation to speak that he could hardly see the dim glory of the scene before him, or the lift of the dark mountains against the stars.

He said: "To a fellow of Jingo's own generation, Judge Tyrrel, it seems that he's just a cheap rascal."

"Ah," the judge said. "A cheap rascal, Wheeler?"

He kept his voice low and caressing. He turned his head a little and seemed to be considering, profoundly, what the young man was saying.

Wheeler Bent was inspired to continue as they paced up and down under the stars.

"A gambler, a notorious gunman, a vagabond. And it shocks me, Judge Tyrrel, to see a man like that received with such great familiarity in your home."

"Ah, does it, Wheeler?" asked the gentle voice of the judge.

"A creature," exclaimed Bent, "capable of taking every advantage! No one knows what rot he's pouring into the ears of Eugenia, just now. A young girl . . . romantic . . . passionate . . . almost unbalanced in her desire to extract from the world the perfume of its pleasures. . . ."

"My dear Wheeler," the judge said, "you talk like a poet."

"When I think of Eugenia . . . of what she is . . . of how she could be wasted if she were allowed to follow the bent of every desire . . . why, it would make anyone poetic, sir."

"Humph!" Judge Tyrrel said, still thoughtful.

"But to have a creature like Jingo in the house!" Bent exclaimed.

"After all," the judge said, "he must be a young man with a good many friends."

"Of course . . . the world is always the same," Wheeler Bent admitted, "and there are bound to be many people who are amused by people who are burning up themselves to make a little, cheap light."

"And yet," said the judge, "he seems to be a fellow of adroitness, good-looking, upstanding, with a good deal of courage."

Wheeler Bent laughed. It was a hollow sound.

"Rogues, gunmen, thieves, blackguards . . . they all have what appears to be courage," Wheeler Bent said. "But the steady moral courage of a good man . . . that's what they lack."

"Well, well, well," said the judge. "What a thoughtful fellow you seem to be, Wheeler."

"Thank you, sir," Wheeler Bent said.

And just then, as they passed a bush, he was aware of something that rose behind it, a dark silhouette that seemed to wave toward him. And the guilty blood ran cold through his veins.

He was glad, a moment later, when the judge said: "Well, I'll turn back inside the house and see how the pair of them is getting on."

"I'll stay out for another moment," Wheeler Bent said. "I . . . er . . . I never saw a more beautiful evening."

"Humph," the judge muttered, and went rapidly back inside the house.

As he came through the big, open doors again, he saw the adventurer, Jingo, rolling a cigarette in the midst of a silence that seemed to have lasted for some moments, at least.

The judge was usually as direct as the attack of a bull terrier. He walked straight up to the pair.

"Well, Gene," he said, "what's the silence all about?"

"Jingo came here full of talk, and you choked it out of him," said the girl gloomily.

"Come, come," Judge Tyrrel said. "Here's the fiery young gallant, the *Don* Quixote, jousting at windmills or the moon, and do you mean to tell me that he hasn't said a word to you? Hasn't he done a thing to make his trip worthwhile?"

"No," said the girl. "He seems to think that just because you've gone out of the room, he has to act like a stump of wood."

The judge whistled softly.

"Jingo," he demanded, "are you one of the boys who are never bad except when the teacher is in the room to watch?"

And then the judge began to laugh heartily. "Sit down, Jingo, and we'll have a talk all together."

Wheeler Bent, in the meantime, had turned back toward the big shrub from behind which the stranger had appeared. As he came near, the form stepped out again.

The voice of Jake Rankin said: "Hello, partner. I just dropped by to report. We got one half of the procession, but the band had already gone by when we arrived."

"Rankin," Wheeler Bent hissed, "are you out of your mind to show yourself so close to the house of Judge Tyrrel? Suppose that someone saw the two of us together, what would be thought?"

"Maybe they'd think that you'd groomed up and started talking to real men," Jake Rankin suggested sourly.

"This way . . . let's get back farther into the brush," whispered Wheeler Bent as he took several steps back. "Here . . . this is better. No one can see us now. Quick, man, tell me what's happened."

Rankin drawled: "Well, we come up with . . ."

"Not so loud," Wheeler Bent pleaded. "Go on."

"We come up with the big walloper they call the Parson, and we snagged him. We've got him tied hand and foot, out yonder. One of my partners has a set of irons in his saddlebag, but we saved them up for Jingo. Understand? Only we don't know where he is."

"He's there . . . he's there!" exclaimed Wheeler Bent. "He's right there inside the house! You've missed him, and let him come through. Heaven knows what will happen now."

"What are you in such a stew about?" Jake Rankin asked.

"I tell you," Wheeler Bent said, "that Jingo is in there. He broke through. In spite of all the men of Judge Tyrrel . . . in spite of you. I've thrown away the money I paid you . . . and Jingo's inside the house. He'll probably run away with the girl now."

"What girl?" asked Jake Rankin.

"What girl? Judge Tyrrel's daughter! That's the girl! What do you think . . . ?"

Wheeler Bent checked himself, for he found his tongue running away. But Jake Rankin seemed to have looked a bit into the future.

He said: "Poaching on you, is he? Dog-gone his young hide, that's what he'd do, too. There ain't anything that he'd overlook in the way of a bet. If he's got a fair chance to talk to that girl, you'd

160

better cash in your checks and get out of the game. About the Parson, yonder . . . you don't want him?"

"Of course not," Wheeler Bent hissed. "What do I care about him?"

"That's what he kind of wondered," Rankin said.

"He wondered? Great heavens, did you mention my name to him?" demanded Wheeler Bent.

"Well, and why not? If you was out after those two *hombres*, we thought that they'd know that you was after them," explained Rankin.

"And you used my name?" groaned Wheeler Bent.

He beat his hands together above his head.

"What of it?" Rankin asked, growling out the words.

"What of it? Simply that his tongue has to be stopped then. Suppose that he ever got to Judge Tyrrel and talked about me? I'd be ruined."

"When you talk about his tongue being stopped," said Rankin, "just what do you mean by that, partner?"

"Stopped? He's got to be kept from speaking!" exclaimed Bent.

"Ah, hum," muttered Rankin. "That's it, is it? Murder is the thing you want, eh?"

"Murder? Who used that word?"

"I did. There ain't any other way of stopping a gent from talking and you know it."

"What do I care how you stop him?" Wheeler Bent said desperately. "I only know that you've balled everything up and confused everything and missed the man I wanted to get . . . and revealed my name. . . ."

He began to groan, making wordless sounds.

"All right," Jake Rankin said. "I'm kind of sorry about it, because he acts and he talks like a real man. But I'm your hired man, just now, and what you say has to go for me. I'll go back and tap the Parson over the head, if you want. I'll bash in his skull for him, and then likely he's going to be silent enough to please even you."

"Bash in his head?" gasped Wheeler Bent.

"If you know a better way, talk it up big and loud," suggested Rankin. "I'm ready enough to listen to it. It ain't what I want to do . . . butcher a man like a beef. It's up to you to talk right out and say what you want."

"I have to leave it in your hands," Wheeler Bent muttered. "I only know that . . . that he mustn't be allowed to talk."

"Yeah, and you could cut his tongue out," Rankin said. "But he'd still have his hands to write with. If you know a better way, you tell me about it."

Wheeler Bent was silent. But the noise of his rapid breathing could be heard.

After a moment Rankin went on: "Now, I'm willing to go ahead and try to do the other half of the job. There's Jingo . . . and you want him, don't you?"

"Yes, yes, yes!" gasped Bent.

"Well, if he's inside the house, you show me the way to him. He's the meat for me, partner. I gotta get at him sometime or other, and why not tonight?"

"Are you out of your wits?" demanded Wheeler Bent. "Don't you know that that house is full of armed men?"

"Well, that's all right, too," Rankin said. "There can be a lot of guns in a crowd . . . and only a few of 'em will go off at the right time."

"You can't take him out of the house," Wheeler Bent said. "There's no use thinking of that."

"Then you go and bring him out to me," suggested Rankin. "How would that suit you?"

"I've got to think," muttered Wheeler Bent, "and my brain's spinning too fast. I can't make it work."

"When a gent can't make his brain work, he'd better start his feet to moving," Rankin remarked. "You go along ahead and do what you can on the job. I'll wait out here."

"Don't wait so near the house," Wheeler Bent said. "Stay farther away."

"All right then. That flat-topped hill over yonder. That's where I'm going to be with the other two. And if you come out there, you can say a last good bye to the Parson . . . poor sucker . . . before we bump him off."

Chapter Twenty

Wheeler Bent, out of breath, staggered, and more or less desperate, got back inside the huge central room of the house and found before his eyes the last picture in the world that he expected or desired to see. For there he saw that Judge Tyrrel was in the midst of hearty laughter and had actually, at that moment, clapped his hand on the shoulder of the detestable vagabond, Jingo. He saw, worse than this if possible, that the girl was looking up at the two with a sheen in her eyes such as Wheeler Bent never had seen in them before.

Young Bent's entire hopes, which, only the day before, had seemed to be based as upon strong granite, now dissolved into vapor. He could hardly see the features of his own settled intentions. All was adrift and at a loss with him.

And he heard Judge Tyrrel say: "But you say that another man came out with you, Jingo?"

"Yes, another man," Jingo said. "The Parson is big enough to make two."

"And where is he now?"

"Out behind a flat-topped hill just near the house. He and I camped there this afternoon and listened to the derricks groaning and watched the loads of hay come in."

"Then he's out there growing hungry. Call him

inside," insisted the judge. "I want to see the sort of a fellow you would team with, Jingo."

"Oh, he'll fill your eye, all right," Jingo said.

"Hello, Wheeler!" called the judge. "Jingo is going out to ask in his friend. You go along to make sure the Parson knows that he'll be welcome in here with us. Hurry along, my lad. Step right along with Jingo."

It was the last invitation that Wheeler Bent wished to accept, but he had to turn, against his will, and walk through the door beside Jingo.

He was never to forget that walk up the hill and what awaited them at the top of the rise.

In the first place, as they stepped out under the bright heavens, Jingo said: "You seem to hate me, Bent. I don't blame you, in a way, but I want to tell you something. If I handed you one on the chin, the other evening, I'm willing to let you have your try at getting even whenever you say so. Right now might be the time to please you. If you can put me down . . . well, I won't be hurrying back inside the house. And if I don't reappear . . . well, your own way might be considerably cleared up for you, old son."

Wheeler Bent looked askance at his companion.

He was the same height. There was hardly a pound of difference in their weight. And Wheeler Bent had been trained in wrestling and boxing since he was a boy. Yet he knew that if there were a fight, he would have no more chance than a fifty-pound dog has against a fifty-pound lynx, or a hundred-pound dog against a hundred-pound panther. He knew that while he was fighting his honest best, there would be a sudden explosion in Jingo, a savage outbursting of energy, an electrical flare of force that would magnify him many times, for a few effective instants.

Wheeler Bent, then, eyed the man beside him as a dog might eye a wolf. Afterward he looked forward to that flat-topped hill toward which Jingo was stepping, for there would be found Jake Rankin and his two assistants with the Parson in their hands. When Bent saw how perfectly his means were matching his ends, he even smiled at the idea of fighting Jingo.

He therefore answered, rather lightly: "Fighting wouldn't be a great help to me or to you. A black eye or a bleeding nose wouldn't decorate the scene any. Besides, I've been bumped on the chin before." He added carelessly: "Just what sort of a fellow is the Parson?"

"The Parson," said Jingo, "is what you might call slow poison. He doesn't start fast, but he keeps on finishing for a long time. He's something. When he wants to, he can be a friend."

"Well, how would you define a friend?" Wheeler Bent asked, glad of the ground they were covering to that flat-topped hill.

"A friend?" Jingo said. "Why, that's the one thing that a man can't get along without."

"A man can't get along without meat and beer," Wheeler Bent stated more lightly than ever.

"He can, though," insisted Jingo. "He can chew leather and eat roots and live on hope. A man can get along without a home or a wife or a child, but he has to have a friend. And the Parson could be that sort of a friend."

"I thought," said Wheeler Bent, "that he was just a big oaf with a face like a horse. I remember seeing him at the dance. Of course, I didn't talk to him."

"Well," said Jingo, "a lot of people can see him without knowing him."

Wheeler Bent looked up at the sky with such a sudden jerk of the head that the stars whirled before his eyes. He thought of himself and how few people in all the world knew him rightly. No one, certainly, knew him well enough to suspect the things that he was planning for this night. This, he determined, would be the one occasion when he would step off the straight and narrow path. But if he could once brush Jingo from his path, he told himself that the rest of his life would flow surely and safely forward to a happy sea. Eugenia would forget the romantic, nameless fellow very shortly. And Wheeler Bent's part in the disappearance of Jingo would never be known.

On the whole, Bent felt satisfied with himself, and he had a sense of extra power. He could understand what was meant in old legends when it was said that a man had sold his soul to the devil. In fact, it seemed to Wheeler Bent that evil walked beside him as an ally, through the dark of this night.

They had come up to the top of the hill, very nearly, when he said in a loud voice: "Well, Jingo, I hope the whole deal will turn out . . ."

They were stepping through the brush at that moment, and there was a sudden exclamation in a deep voice that seemed to rise out of the ground.

"Jingo! Look out!"

Jingo leaped to the side as he heard the exclamation, and as he sprang, there was the instant sheen of a gun in his hand. But behind the brush, several dim forms were rising. Something cut the air with a hissing whisper, and Wheeler Bent saw the noose of a rope—a movement rather than an image on the eye—fall over Jingo. The rope was drawn taut with a jerk that tumbled Jingo on the ground. The gun slithered away out of his hand among the leaves, and the dark forms hurled themselves on him.

Even in the tingling fear of that crisis, Wheeler Bent noticed that there was no outcry from Jingo. And that seemed strange. He would have expected the snarling of a fighting wildcat. Instead, there was only the noise of scuffling and the gasping and grunting of laboring men.

Then a perfect silence followed. Jingo lay on the ground, trussed hand and foot.

"That was easier than I figured it would be," said the voice of Jake Rankin as he stood up again.

"Yeah," another responded, "but if the Parson had yipped a quarter of a second sooner, it wouldn't've been easier for a couple of us. We'd've been too dead to worry about how we went out. That's my way of seeing it."

"Get the irons on him," Rankin ordered.

One of the men stepped away.

"Give us a patch of light," went on Rankin.

One of his helpers struck a match and kindled, with the little crackling flame, a handful of dry twigs. It burned up like a torch. The gentle wind leaned the fire to one side, and, in the utter silence, Wheeler Bent could hear the soft fluttering of the flame.

By that light, he saw the Parson, his immense body swathed in rope, his hands tied behind his back. To Jingo it seemed a wonder that ropes that could hold a horse were able to hold a man so powerful. He believed that he should be hearing a series of loud bursting noises as the ropes flew to pieces and the giant sprang up to battle.

A man with the pointed face of a rat and bright little hungry eyes came from down the hill, carrying a jingle of irons.

He kneeled beside Jingo and began to fit the irons on him.

And a sudden excess of joy rushed over the

heart of Wheeler Bent, making him exclaim: "You've done a great job, Rankin! You're a real man-catcher."

"Now that I've got him, where do you want him delivered?" Rankin asked.

"Wait a moment, boys," said the calm voice of Jingo. "Is Bent behind this job?"

"Behind it? He *is* it!" exclaimed the Parson. "The dirty pup hired Rankin to get us. They grabbed me here, from behind. I was watching the house, Jingo. I wouldn't've thought of something coming from behind. And they dropped right onto me. They dropped out of the sky on me, and tied me up in a bundle."

"And Wheeler Bent is the paymaster, eh?" Jingo said softly. "Oh, I'm a soft-headed fool."

Bent came closer. His body was quivering. There had been electric fear in him, then triumph, and now he found himself wanting to enjoy sufferings.

"You see," he said as he stood over Jingo, "what a fool I would have been to fight you?"

Jingo looked up at him with a smile such as Bent had never endured before from any man.

A savage impulse made Bent lean and strike the flat of his hand into the face of Jingo. The blow made a loud, popping sound. That sound and the feel of the flesh under his fingers sent long thrills through the body of Wheeler Bent.

He drew back his hand again, and suspended the

weight of it, ready. He was thinking of what effect this scene would make upon Judge Tyrrel and upon the daughter of the judge, if they could look in on it. He enjoyed considering that effect. It seemed to Wheeler Bent that there was one simple solution to all the problems of life, and that was to have at one's beck and call trustworthy men, savage, wolfish men, who obey because it is worth their while.

These were the things that were in the mind of Wheeler Bent. He was ready to strike the face of Jingo again, because the smile continued there. But his arm was caught by Jake Rankin.

And Rankin said: "Don't sock that *hombre* while he's down. He ain't that kind. He's a straight up-and-up fighter. Don't poke him in the face again while his hands are tied."

"I'll do what I want with him. I've bought him and paid for him," Wheeler Bent gasped, an uncontrollable anger brewing in him.

His own voice was new to him. It was huskier and pitched on a deeper note than of old.

"Yeah, and that's all right," Jake Rankin said. "But don't sock him again when he's down. I don't like it."

Jake Rankin did not like it? Well, in the future days, when the fortune of Judge Tyrrel was at his command, he would have men who would not dare to question him on how he lifted his hand.

But for the present?

171

There was something in Jake Rankin's manner of speaking that made Wheeler Bent step back though an unsatisfied appetite was still raging in him. Strange to say, he felt the throb of a recurrent pain on the side of his jaw, where the fist of Jingo had gone home the night before. He knew, suddenly, that he could enjoy shredding away the body of this man to small bits and pieces. He wanted nothing in the world so much as a chance to wring one shriek of agony from Jingo. Above all, he saw in the eyes of Jingo a perfect understanding of him, and that maddened Wheeler Bent more than ever.

He could hardly hear the voice of Rankin, saying: "What's to happen to this pair of *hombres*?"

"Take them . . . somewhere. . . . No, hold them," Wheeler Bent ordered. "I want . . . to see Jingo . . . again."

Brutal words came to him, but he kept them back.

Rankin said: "Put him out of the way and hold him? You dunno what you're talking about. But I understand this *hombre*, old son. I understand him like a book." Rankin kept on nodding his head. "You can't keep a pair like this. You can't keep 'em long, I mean. They'll find ways of busting loose. A pair like this . . . you'd need ten men to watch 'em, day and night. You gotta do something else with 'em."

"What do you mean?" Wheeler Bent snapped.

"Yeah . . . and you know what I mean," answered Rankin.

The cruel fury swelled in the throat of Wheeler Bent again.

"Then . . . bash in their heads here and now!" he hissed.

Rankin looked at him curiously.

Boyd, the rat-faced man, and Oliver, the bull-dog, drew close to the shoulders of their chief and stared at Wheeler Bent. They seemed to understand very intimately what they saw there.

"Bump off the pair of 'em right here," said Rankin, "where we leave a lot of footprints and stuff like that behind us? No, Bent. I ain't such a fool. We gotta take 'em to another place. And that's where we'll finish 'em. Got any good place in mind?"

And suddenly Wheeler Bent saw the place. He seemed to have known it from the first. Above the house, where the cañon of the creek narrowed, where the water gathered headway as through a flume, there were many great boulders strewn about, and the whole place looked as though it had been produced by an explosion that had rent through the base of the mountain and left vast fragments scattered here and there.

"Go up the cañon of the creek," Wheeler Bent said. "And . . . and hold them there for a while. Go there, will you? Up the cañon of the creek. You'll come to a place where the water'll chew up their bodies against the rocks. Chew them up so small that there won't be a trace left afterward. There'll be moonlight, a little later. You'll be able to see what you're doing. Take them there . . . and hold them."

"Why hold 'em?" Rankin asked, still staring curiously.

"Because I've got to go back to the house now, and explain that Jingo has gone away . . . with the Parson. And I won't be able to tell where they've gone."

He laughed hoarsely.

"Hold them up the cañon, and when I get a chance, I'll come up there and see the last of them. I've got to make sure. I've got to see what happens."

Chapter Twenty-One

Wheeler Bent went straight back to the house. He paused only an instant at the door and, when he entered the room, he was laughing.

"Where's Jingo? Where's the Parson?" Judge Tyrrel asked.

Wheeler Bent dissolved the heartiness of his laughter into a mere chuckling sound.

"There's a wild pair for you, Judge Tyrrel," he said. "When I got out there, I saw the Parson, looking as big as a house, and told him that you wanted him in for supper. 'That's all right,' said the Parson, and pulled Jingo aside, muttering something at his ear. Jingo seemed excited. 'Where are they?' he asked. At that, the Parson whispered something else. 'We'll go and get them now. We'll burn 'em up,' Jingo said to him.

"And with that, he jumped a horse and simply sang out to me . . . 'Tell the judge that I forgot I had a previous engagement.' And he and the Parson went galloping off. They're as wild as a pair of hawks."

"Hawks are not half as wild," the judge commented. "Well, I was young myself, in the old days, but I was never half as young as that. What do you think of it, Eugenia?"

175

The girl stood by the fireplace where the uneven flooding of the light threw continual shadows over her face. She said nothing at all in answer to her father but looked straight at Wheeler Bent as though she were thinking about him rather than seeing his face.

"What is it?" asked the judge. "Come now, Eugenia. What's in that brain of yours?"

She shook her head.

"I was simply wondering," she said, "what might be the point of Wheeler's joke."

"Wheeler's joke?" Judge Tyrrel asked.

"Well," she said, "I don't think that Jingo is galloping anywhere, just now."

"Great Scott, Gene," Wheeler Bent said, "what do you mean?"

"I don't know," she answered. "I'm just doing a little wondering."

Wheeler Bent was silent. He stared at the girl with half-closed eyes, for suddenly it came over him that Jingo was as like this girl as though he had been born her twin. Their coloring was different, but they had the same slender rounding beauty of body, the same look of swift-handed surety, the same sheen of the eyes, the smile that meant nothing but delight in life. Now that the idea had come to Wheeler Bent, by looking at the girl, he was able to conjure up the ghost of Jingo beside her. And he was mortally glad that the last hours of Jingo were now ending.

Only a little time from this, and if he were seen, it would have to be his ghost, indeed.

Not long after this, a procession moved up the cañon of the creek—Jake Rankin riding first with his Winchester balanced across the bow of his saddle, and behind him came the Parson with his hands still lashed behind his back, his feet tied under the belly of his mare, and her lead rope fastened to Rankin's saddle.

After them came Jingo with the irons on his wrists and on his ankles. Therefore he had to ride aside in his saddle, and he was very simply secured by means of a lariat whose slip noose was about his throat, the other end of the rope being fastened about the horn of his saddle. If he slipped from his place on the restless horse, he would be quickly throttled, and since his hands were not free, he had only his sense of balance to preserve him in the saddle. This had been the device of Jake Rankin.

"You been used to walking a tightrope all your life, partner," he had said to Jingo. "You might just as well continue to keep on walking one right up to the very end, as I see it."

"Of course I might," Jingo had answered.

On either side of Jingo, watching with keen eyes lest he should free himself by some stroke of magic, rode Boyd, the rat-faced man, and Oliver, the bulldog. They kept smiling—the sort of smiles that stretch the lips without wrinkling the eyes. They felt, when they looked at their prisoner, that they were eating the food of the gods.

The moon was up now. And since the cañon turned straight toward the east, the pale light flooded the ravine and gilded the nakedness of the rocks as though rain were falling and every stone were polished with wetness.

"Here we are," Jake Rankin said at last. "This is the spot that Bent picked out. I gotta say that *hombre* has an eye in his head. Look around you, Jingo. Here's where you pass out, brother."

Jingo took the advice and looked around him. They were in the midst of a junk heap, and the boulders were the junk. It looked as though some incredible stream of water had blasted a way through the mountain range as the jet from a hose cuts through a light heap of dust. That force seemed to have cleared the mountains in a clean-cut line, and here were scattered the fragments—rocks the size of a house.

The creek that ran at their feet was a thin trickle left over after the deluge. The moonlight showed the rapidity with which the whirlings drifted down the course of the creek, and from the troubled surface of the stream, mild flickerings of moonlight kept at play over the rocks, like the ghost of a dancing fire.

Just below this wider point, the creek gathered in a narrow flume that sucked in the water with an audible sound. For a considerable distance the current shot through a deep decline and hurled out on the other side among more rocks, where the water was shattered to a white froth.

"Look at it, Jingo," Jake Rankin declared. "This here is a regular machine. Regular combination harvester. We tap you birds over the head and drop you into this here end of the run, and the water pulls you right down the chute to where the machinery chews you up fine. There ain't going to be no testimony left. Maybe a button or a fingernail might float ashore, somewhere farther down the line. But not much. Not enough to start nobody thinking."

"It's certainly a surprise to me," Jingo said.

"What's a surprise?" asked Jake Rankin.

He undid the lariat from the pommel of the saddle, as he spoke, and allowed Jingo to slide, with a jangling of irons, to the ground.

Now Jingo looked around him again, his head held cheerfully high.

"It's a surprise to run across so many brains in a fellow with a mustache like Wheeler Bent's," Jingo said.

Jake Rankin, laughing, made answer: "You never can tell. He'll change when he gets older. There's some men that change their mugs the way pretty girls do when they put on ten years. This bird, Wheeler Bent, he's going to look like what he is in a little while. And when he does, the snakes are going to run to get away from his poison. Sit down, Jingo, and make yourself at home. You'll be gone before you know it."

"Thanks," Jingo said. "This rock was made to order for me."

He sat down not far from the edge of the water, while the Parson sat down cross-legged on a patch of pebbles nearby, with his back against a rock.

"Look, Parson," Jake Rankin said with something like kindness in his voice; "you got your back up ag'in' the edge of that rock. You ain't going to be comfortable there."

"I like it better this way," the Parson assured Rankin. "I need something sharp to dig into me, because that's the only way I'll be sure that I ain't dreaming."

"What's the matter?" asked Rankin. "Are you taking this hard, old son?"

"Me?" the Parson asked. "Sure, I ain't taking it hard. But it's kind of like a dream. It's so like a dream that I'm going to be dropping away to sleep before long. I mean . . . the idea that you gents could've got Jingo and me so dead easy."

"Yeah," agreed Jake Rankin. "I looked for a lot more trouble." He looked at the rat and the bulldog and said: "Sit down, boys, and keep your eyes on things, will you?"

Boyd and Oliver sat down, facing Jingo. They had an occasional eye for the Parson, but, in spite of the irons that held Jingo, he was their main concern.

"We oughta get the job over with," Boyd suggested, making his eyes smaller and brighter than ever.

"What's eating you, kid?" asked Jake Rankin.

"Nothing. Except that Jingo looks so cheerful that it kind of gets on my nerves. It kind of gets me worried. We'd oughta finish him off right now."

"Quit being worried," Jake Rankin snapped.

He added, as he fished a key out of a pocket: "Look at this here. Them are old-fashioned irons, and Jingo ain't going to get clear of them unless they're sawed through or unlocked. And so there go his chances of any funny work."

He tossed the key into the air. It flickered in the moonlight, made a spark of brightness on the surface of the water, and was gone.

"Yeah," Boyd said, "but suppose that this *hombre* passes his hands out through the handcuffs. I've heard of that."

"You've heard of folks that could make their hands smaller than their wrists? I've heard of it, too," Jake Rankin said. "But not hands like Jingo's that have some muscle in 'em. Jingo, you ever seen a growed-up man that could slip a pair of handcuffs?"

"One," Jingo answered after a moment of thought.

181

"Yeah, and maybe not more'n one in the world," answered Rankin. "But you boys keep on watching Jingo, and the more nervouser you are, the closer you'll watch him. We can't finish off the job now."

"Why not?" Oliver asked.

"Because our boss wants to see the job done," answered Rankin. "Don't forget that Wheeler Bent wants to see these *hombres* wiped out. And he's paying plenty good money to see the party, too. And suppose we pass this pair into the machine before he comes . . . he might say that we've only turned 'em loose in the hills. No, like it or not, we gotta wait."

Boyd grunted. He pulled out a big Colt, laid it on his knee, and pointed it straight at Jingo.

"All right," Boyd said finally. "We're going to keep you here till the boss shows up. But if you make any funny move . . . well, he's going to have to see you dead instead of alive. Savvy?"

"I follow your drift," said Jingo.

He even smiled as he spoke, and then, looking past Boyd, he was aware that the shoulders of the Parson were stirring slowly up and down, and his elbows seemed to be inching up and down little by little, also.

He thought at first, with a shock, that it was mere nervousness, but the regularity of the motion convinced him that it was something more.

Then he could understand.

The Parson had not chosen to put his back against the sharp edge of that rock for any casual reason. He wanted the ragged corner of the boulder to use as a saw for scraping through the strands of the ropes that held his wrists together behind his back.

Chapter Twenty-Two

Time went on strangely in the house of Judge Tyrrel. The judge told an excellent story of his early mining days, and how, for ten years, he had grubstaked a gloomy old sourdough who turned in not a single penny worth of profit.

"Still I had faith in him," said the judge. "He was quite a geologist. He was a good, patient worker. And I kept grubstaking him for a decade. Finally my patience gave out. I told him that I was giving him supplies for the last time. Well, out he went, and came back inside of a month with the Lodestar Mine in his pocket, so to speak. I thought at first that it was a queer break of luck. But afterward I found out the truth.

"That old sourdough had spotted the lode during the second year he was working for me, but he wouldn't tell of the strike so long as he could get grubstakes out of me. Why? Because he didn't really want gold. He simply wanted the hunt for it. And he wanted to ramble around alone through the hills. When he confessed what he had done to me, he added that he never knew of any luck to come to a prospector who made a big strike. A strike would just poison him if he made a lot of money. 'Gold poisoning,' he said, was what most prospectors died of.

"I took so much out of the Lodestar that his share made the old fellow rich, but he was always gloomy, always expecting something to happen. What did happen was that a woman got her hands on him, married him, and then gave him such a devil of a time that he signed everything over to her as a way of getting a divorce.

"Three years after finding the Lodestar he was broke and happy again, and steering a burro through the mountains in search of another strike. He never found another. I kept him on a pension. But he was always happy. He used to say that he was the only man in the world that ever recovered from a bad case of gold poisoning."

Wheeler Bent was able to laugh fluently at this tale, but the girl showed not the slightest amusement. She remained in her chair by the fire, regarding nothingness with far-journeying eyes.

Now and again her glance narrowed a little, and that was always when she turned her gaze on the handsome face and the sparkling little golden mustache of Wheeler Bent.

For Wheeler Bent was changed. He was not the young man she had known so well in other days. There was a keenness about him, a suppressed excitement, the attitude of one who talks casually, but waits for the curtain to rise on an important stage.

The judge came over to her suddenly and stood

before her with his hands clasped behind his back, while he teetered slowly back and forth.

"Now you tell me, Eugenia," he said. "What is the matter?"

She shook her head.

"Is this about Jingo?" asked the judge.

"Yes," she said.

She saw a quick shudder run through the body of Wheeler Bent. Perhaps that was not altogether strange. To all intents and purposes, she had been as good as engaged to Wheeler Bent. Now he was hardly more than a stranger. Yes, something more, but not in a pleasant sense.

Her father said: "Tell me what you're thinking?"

"I can't," she said.

"Why not?"

"It isn't thinking, really," she said. "It's only a feeling."

"What sort?"

"Oh . . . that something has gone wrong."

"With Jingo?"

"Yes."

"Perhaps something has. Perhaps he's gone galloping . . . to get a broken neck," the judge said angrily. "My dear, you have a fancy for a romantic, worthless gunman, and you'll laugh at the memory of him in another month."

"Excuse me," Wheeler Bent said, rising from his chair. "I'll trot along to bed. Good night, Judge. Good night, Eugenia."

When he shook hands with her, she looked squarely at him, amazed by the alteration that appeared in his face when he was close to her. His expression was set in a new way. There was about him the look of one who is prepared and nerved for a great effort.

After he had left the room, the judge said: "I suppose he was right to get out of the way, but he had a right to hear us talk. He's been rather close to you in the past, Eugenia."

"I don't think he ever will be again," said the girl.

"No," agreed the judge slowly. "I don't suppose that he ever will be again."

"Why are you so sure?" she asked.

"For your reason, I imagine," said the judge. "Because this lad Jingo has come galloping into our family circle."

"That's the reason," agreed the girl.

"You can't believe that he would be wild enough to gallop off and just send back a message to you?" the judge said.

She shook her head.

"It's the nature of the message," she answered. "He might have said other things. He wouldn't have said that."

"That he had forgotten that he had a previous engagement?" the judge repeated, chuckling.

"He wouldn't be rude," she said. "If he had to lie, he would tell a polite lie."

"He has the reputation of being pretty rough," the judge said.

"He has the reputation of liking a fight," she said. "Rudeness is a different thing."

"No matter what you think," said the judge, "the fact remains that he *did* make that remark. That was the message he gave Wheeler Bent, and that Wheeler gave you."

She shook her head in silence.

The judge exclaimed: "Gene, you don't think that Wheeler would lie to you?"

She hesitated for a long moment.

Her father kept waiting, leaning over her a little. Then she said: "Yes. I'm sure that he lied."

The judge took a step back and frowned at her.

"That's serious," he said.

"I know it's serious," she agreed.

"What do you think is in the air?"

"Trouble," she said shortly.

"Gene," muttered the judge, "this fellow Jingo has upset you a good deal. You're taking him pretty seriously."

"So are you," she answered.

He started. But suddenly he nodded and answered: "Yes, I'm taking him seriously. Because . . . well, because I don't think there's anything wrong about him . . . nothing that wouldn't wash off, so to speak."

He began to walk up and down. Then he took a chair and remained staring at the fire.

She stood up, saying: "I'm going upstairs."

He bade her good night absently.

She went to the door, paused there to look back at him, and felt with a sudden outrush of affection that there were few problems in the world that she could not work out with his assistance. But on this night—well, things might happen that could not be put straight in the morning.

She hurried up the stairs, resolved on speaking with Wheeler Bent, but when she rapped at his door, twice and loudly, there was no answer. She pushed the door open. A lamp burned in front of the window, as though to give assurance that Bent was in the room, but he was gone.

Chapter Twenty-Three

That he should be gone from his room was not very strange, after all. She kept telling herself this, and yet her heart was beating faster and faster. She told herself that she would wait there in the room until he returned. There were a few questions that she had to ask of him. So she went to the open window and looked out at the night, now brightening under the rising moon.

That light showed the shingles on the sloping roof of the shed just beneath the window. It showed the grand forms of the mountains against the horizon, and it showed the beginning of the trail that advanced toward the upper hills. On that trail she saw a man running, head down with labor as he took the grade. And that man was Wheeler Bent!

A voice seemed to shout into her ear that he must be stopped, and that she must find out where he was bound.

She was out of the room in an instant, and down the stairs and through the back door. It was wide open, as Bent must have left it in going from the house. She hurried out beyond the shed. Wheeler Bent was no longer in sight on the first lap of the trail, but he would be in view and in earshot, she was sure, if she ran up to the first angling bend of it. For beyond that the trail went up as steeply as a ladder, and he would be climbing more slowly.

So she ran to the first turn. But Bent was not in sight.

She cupped her hands at her lips and shouted on a high-pitched, wailing note: "Wheeler! Wheeler Bent!"

The echo beat back at her, a flat, dull, quick sound. And all at once her heart was hammering and thundering and choking her as it swelled within her. She ran up the sharp slope of the way, staggering with haste and with the steepness. So she gained the next level of the trail—and saw it winding easily before her, but still without a trace of Bent upon it.

She was too breathless to call for him again instantly. She looked back, with the thought of returning to the house and giving up this wild-goose chase. But as she stared at the moonlit picture of the house and the big barns beside it, with the hay wagons standing nearby, like awkward, black-ribbed skeletons, she heard the mourning voice of the creek rising out of its valley, and a new panic came over her. It was as though the voice spoke directly to her.

She ran on again, around several turns of the trail. Then, when there was still no trace of Wheeler Bent, she cupped her hands at her lips and shouted his name once more.

"Wheeler Bent! Oh, Wheeler!"

She got not even an echo for an answer, only the dull roaring of her own blood in her ears. And then, suddenly, she hoped that he had not heard her, for she remembered at that moment the expression that had been beginning in his eyes before he said good night to her and to her father. If that expression grew, it would not be a thing for her to face by night.

It was better, perhaps, simply to follow along in the hope of discovering what Bent aimed his course for. Since he had gone on foot, his destination could not be very far away.

But when she came to the division of the trail, where one branch of it ran into the farther hills and the other half extended down into the upper ravine of the creek, she paused for a long moment. In the upper ravine there was nothing to be found but naked rocks and the rushing of the stream. And yet the voice of the water now called to her more intimately than before.

Yonder in the ravine, Jingo was doing his best to keep the attention of Jake Rankin and the two men who helped Jake keep watch. For, while Jingo entertained the three, the Parson was still busily at work, rubbing his ropes, with all the backward strength of his arms, against the edge of the boulder where he leaned.

If there had not come to the ears of the Parson, now and again, the muted sound of parting of strands of the rope, he would not have continued his labor, it seemed certain. Moreover, there was something in his huge, ugly face that was like a hope. He kept on stealthily, his shoulders and elbows working imperceptibly, except to a keen eye like that of Jingo.

He even saw the moment when the blood began to run out from the chafed arms of the Parson. It was a mere darkening of the surface of the rock, barely visible from the side. But it increased rapidly. It looked as though the Parson, in his labors, had chafed through some artery in his wrist. After all, the vital life was hidden close under the skin in that part of the body.

It was even a possibility that the Parson had chosen this moment of letting the life run out of his body rather than waiting for a blow on the head and then that horrible death in the grinding mill of the cataract that muttered in the distance.

But it needed only a moment for Jingo to decide that he was wrong. Whatever was in the mind of the Parson, he would not give up hope until the last instant.

So Jingo went on with the story of the brindle steer that Hugh Wilson had bought from the rustlers, and what followed in the track of the steer, and how Laughing Dan McGillicuddy had called on Jingo to come and join the Dance of the Brindle Steer up there in Lawson County. It was a good story, particularly after the point where Jingo joined and speeded up the dance.

Little Boyd, with the rat-face, kept making small snarling noises of delight, and Oliver grunted with pleasure now and again.

Boyd said finally: "Jake, it's almost kind of too bad to bump off a gent like Jingo. It'd be kind of a game to ride a trail with this here *hombre*."

Jake Rankin answered: "I'll tell you boys something. Jingo takes things easy, like a crook. He likes a fight as much as a crook. He likes a change as much as a crook. But he *ain't* a crook. And all you'd get out of him after a while would be a dose of lead between the ribs someday. But, leaving all of that out of it, I got a brother back home that's been plastered by him. And when I get back to town, I wanna tell my brother something that'll make him sit up in bed and take an interest in life ag'in."

That ended the argument.

Boyd muttered: "Aw, I was just talking. Go on, Jingo. What happened after you got the greaser cornered?"

"Wait a minute," broke in Rankin thoughtfully. "Seems like Jingo was talking to kill time."

"Sure he is," answered Boyd. "He's talking to keep his mind off the noise of the water."

They were silent for an instant, listening to the cool, dashing sound of the cataract, and the small muttering of the echoes.

Then Rankin said: "All right. But Jingo's got something in his head, mind you."

"Brains," suggested Boyd, "but they'll stop working pretty soon."

The attention of the crew was so totally fixed upon Jingo by this time that the Parson, with a slight nod of understanding at Jingo, began to saw on his ropes with a larger and more reckless motion of his arms. And the dark stain spread farther over the surface of the rock, and the gleam of the coursing blood was so plain to the eyes of Jingo that he wondered how the others could fail, even at the first casual glance, to mark the thing.

"Hey!" Boyd cried suddenly. "There's somebody coming. Jake, what we going to do?"

"Wait a minute," said Rankin.

He stepped back among the boulders.

Jingo could distinctly hear the thump and the grinding of heels on the rocks as someone came on the run toward them.

Then Rankin stepped back into view, saying: "Sure, there's somebody coming, and it's the boss. Jingo, you and the Parson won't have long to wait."

Out through the tangle of the great rocks came Wheeler Bent a moment later. He was panting from the hard effects of his run, and he stood there, leaning his hand against a big stone for an instant, and getting his breath.

But his smile of satisfaction had begun even before he was able to speak.

At last he gasped: "I was afraid . . . every step I took along the way . . . that I wouldn't find you fellows around here. I was afraid that something must've gone wrong."

Oliver said: "Three hearts that beat as one, boss. What could go wrong with us?"

"That's right," agreed Boyd. "Nothing could go wrong. We got him in irons, and the key's been throwed away. What could go wrong?"

Wheeler Bent nodded. Then he went over to Jingo and leaned above him.

"How goes it?" he asked.

"Better than you dream," Jingo said. "Thanks."

"Better?" Wheeler Bent snapped with a suspicious side glance at Jake Rankin.

"Sure, a lot better," said Jingo.

"He's just talking," Jake Rankin said. "You can't put him down till you put him dead. He's got that kind of a tongue. It's gotta keep going."

"Well," said Wheeler Bent, "I'll tell you that the girl and her father are all worried about you, Jingo. You'll be sorry to hear about that, I guess."

Jingo said nothing. He merely bent back his head and looked calmly up into the face of Wheeler Bent.

"She's rather tragic about it," went on Bent. "But she'll get over all that. And when she's over it, there'll be a good friend . . . an old friend, a tried-and-true friend . . . waiting to take her to the altar. Eh?"

He laughed.

Jingo said: "She's seen a man, old son. She'll never make that mistake. Not that way."

"Who you guys talking about?" demanded Boyd curiously.

"Nothing you know about," Wheeler Bent answered, looking annoyed. "Just a little secret. We might call it a family secret, Jingo, eh?"

"We might call it that," Jingo said.

"Well," said Wheeler Bent, "the time's come, boys."

"How d'you want us to go about it?" demanded Jake Rankin.

"Pop them over the head and then throw them in the water. That's good enough for me." He added after a slight pause: "Wait a minute. I'll do the trick on Jingo. I'd enjoy doing it, as a matter of fact."

Wheeler Brent took out a revolver as he spoke, and grasped it firmly and swayed the heavy gun up and down, ready for the stroke. That was the instant that Jingo heard a distinct popping sound as a big strand of the Parson's rope gave way.

Chapter Twenty-Four

That sound of the parting rope strand was no doubt partially covered by the noise the creek was continually making, yet it seemed very strange to Jingo that every one of the four men did not whirl suddenly around. Perhaps it was because the thing plucked at the strings of his heart that it seemed to him certain that the four must have heard it, and that they were masking their knowledge.

Or perhaps it was the savage, panting voice of Wheeler Bent that kept the attention of the rest. They could not see the great arms of the Parson swing clear from behind his back. Tangled fragments of rope hung down from his wrists, and from the frayed ends of the rope the blood was dripping.

"You're a bright fellow, Jingo," Wheeler Bent was saying. "You're so bright that perhaps you'll be able to say a good prayer for yourself . . . out loud. Mind you, you'll live just as long as it takes you to say the prayer . . . out loud."

There was laughter trying to get into the rage and savage delight of his voice.

Jingo looked up into the face of Bent and saw the beast in it. The eyes were changed. The flesh was furrowing up around them and covering them with shadow.

Jingo saw the hand that weighted the revolver above him and the strain of the knuckles in grasping the gun. He saw, also, that forward sway of the freed arms of the Parson in the background, and something that was more important to him than anything else, though it was simply another study in facial expression. For the Parson had not the look of guilty fear that a man wears when he is hoping to free himself from an immediate peril and then dodge away. Rather, he looked like one who is shaking off impediments so that he can charge into battle.

That was the grim expression of the Parson as he brought out a hunting knife and with it slashed through the ropes that tied his legs. Almost with the same gesture he was rising to his feet. Why, the mere shadow of his coming, the mere wind and stir of the rising of the giant should have made those others turn toward him.

But they did not turn. They were too utterly fascinated by the words and the actions of Wheeler Bent, and the murder that he was weighing in his hand above the head of Jingo. There was interest and some cruel satisfaction in their faces, and a sick distaste, as well. Only the butcher was going to enjoy the actual process of the butchery.

"Now you tell me, and stop sneering up at me!" Wheeler Bent cried. "You tell me your last prayer . . . you hear? I want to know it. I want to hear how you'll beg and ask for mercy."

"Don't be a fool," Jake Rankin said.

"Then he gets it now!" shouted Wheeler Bent. And he swung the heavy revolver to the full stretch of his arm.

The Parson struck them then. He came in with his arms spread out wide. He looked like a father about to sweep up his family of little boys. Such was the vast size of him. And as he came running in, bent to the shock, Jingo could still see the blood dripping fast from the rope ends that festooned his wrists.

He struck them all in a heap. All except Boyd. The rat-faced man had the least bit of instinct working in him, the electric thing that made him leap suddenly to the side, and the reaching hand of the Parson just swept by and missed him with its clutch.

The others went down in a crashing, squirming, shouting heap on top of Jingo. A hand reached in for him and jerked him out with the resistless sway of some great steam derrick. The hand caught his clothes at the breast and nearly ripped them off his back. He came clear of the heap in time to see Boyd shoot a bullet right into the body of the Parson.

Jingo had time to say to himself that that was the end. It was all he had time to say before the arm of the Parson flew out with the walking-beam weight of his shoulder behind it. His fist spatted against the face of Boyd. It seemed as though there were no weight to the head of the rat-faced man. It seemed as though he would not, therefore, receive any real damage from the blow—no more than a light image stuffed with sawdust, say.

His head flicked back—so far back that he looked headless for an instant. Then he was falling.

That living heap of men was surging up around Jingo as he saw Boyd knocked flat. Something glinted—a revolver in the hand of Wheeler Bent. Jingo got that gun in his two manacled hands as the Parson swung his weight up and over his shoulder, like a sack of bran. Jingo lay on his stomach over the vast, board-like bones of the Parson's shoulder, with a snaky cushioning of muscles to make his resting place easier.

He saw, as the Parson sprang away with him, how Boyd lay on his back, with his head supported against the base of a boulder. His neck looked as though it were broken. His eyes were open, empty. His face no longer looked like the face of a rat. It looked simply like an incomplete thing—a mangled thing.

Jingo saw that and knew that Boyd would give no other person any trouble, not on this night, at least. But Boyd was not worth noticing, compared with the upspring of three wildcat forms out of the heap of humanity that the Parson had struck to the earth. He had only needed two or three seconds to strike, grab Jingo, and leap away among the shadows of the boulders. He had pounced as a tiger might spring. But Jingo heard a wild yell that could not come out of any throat except that of Jake Rankin. He saw Jake come up off the ground as though flung from a springboard.

And right at him, Jingo fired the first shot from the gun that he held in both hands.

He missed his target. He knew that he had missed. To fire with both hands ironed together was no easy trick. Besides, lying on the shoulder of the Parson as he ran was no smoother than lying across the back of a trotting horse. That was why Jingo missed an easy shot at five yards. Then the raw, ragged edges and the faces of the boulders came in between. He could not see anything more. He could only hear the monstrous yelling of Jake Rankin, like a beast driven mad with a torturing disappointment. Jake was like a cat that had played with a mouse until the mouse escapes. He was simply screaming in a blinding passion.

Aye, and running. Wheeler Bent's voice was shouting something. Yes, something about more money to them all if they caught the runaways.

Well, they would be caught, all right. Jingo was sure enough. The Parson was a giant, but, after all, he had not the strength of a horse. Not even the Parson had as much strength as that. He had, besides, a bullet somewhere in his huge body. Jingo had seen the bullet strike. He had heard the thud of it, like a blow on a filled barrel. In a moment or two the Parson had to curl up and quit.

Jingo said at his ear, while the Parson raced with immense strides among the rocks: "Chuck me, Parson. They've got us now. Chuck me. You can save yourself then. Get away. Then start on their trail and finish them all, Parson."

The arm with which the Parson was gripping him, holding him in place on that vast shoulder, was like the weight of a beam. It was crushing the breath out of Jingo. A little more pressure from that arm was his only answer, as though the Parson had felt him slipping.

To Jingo, suddenly, to die was nothing. When two friends face it together, what is death more than a joke?

He had a split part of a second for that thought, and then he saw Oliver sprint around the side of a boulder as big as a house and come right at them. Oliver had a gun out. He was leaning so far forward with speed that he seemed with each step barely to save himself from falling on his face. He was shooting every time his foot struck the ground.

Jingo saved his own bullet through half a count, to get the sway of the Parson's running balanced in his mind, his eye, his manacled hands. Then he fired.

Oliver kept right on running, but he started falling, too. His arms stretched out. The gun slid down from one of them, like a drop of liquid brilliant with moonlight. Oliver struck the ground. He turned a somersault. He lay bunched like a wounded spider, his legs drawn up, his arms wrapped around himself.

Wheeler Bent and Jake Rankin were in full view for an instant. Then they were out of sight.

The Parson had dodged behind another of those vast fragments of mountain, and now he dropped to one knee and let Jingo slump off his shoulder.

The thumping and grinding of footfalls sped past them.

Jingo stood up with his back against the rock, the gun still clutched with both hands. He and the Parson were on a little strip of gravel beach, at the edge of the waters of the creek. The moon shadow fell thickly over them, but the light of the moon danced up like the ghostly image of firelight and threw from the stirring face of the creek a changing, wavering, dim pattern over the boulder and over the Parson.

He leaned his shoulder and his head against the rock. He was stifling the noise of his panting and the groaning of his pain, so that his face was made frightful by the struggle. He had both of his immense hands pressed against his side, where the bullet had struck him.

The noise of Rankin and Wheeler Bent was gone out in the distance. There was only the smooth sound of the creek as it slipped among the rocks and the cool dashing of it far away, at the end of the flume. There were these sounds and the small throttling noises that came out of the distorted mouth of the Parson.

But he was not an ugly mask to Jingo. Instead, he was something more than handsome. If Jingo lived to tell of that night, he knew he would always remember every day of his life, with awe and a great swelling of the heart, the exact look of the Parson. Because that was the way a man looked when he was dying for a friend.

It was not the face only that was distorted. The great bare throat of the Parson was swollen with the might of his effort.

Jingo laid the gun on the ground, filled his cupped hands with water, and dashed it into the face of the Parson, and the Parson suddenly seemed able to breathe.

He closed his eyes. His mouth was open. His jaw worked as he bit at the air and swallowed it and regained life.

Jingo, on his knees, pulled the hands of the Parson from the place of the wound.

The whole side of the giant was sopping and running with blood. He ought to be dead, Jingo told himself. Surely any other man in the world would be dead.

He caught hold of the shirt and tore it from the Parson's body. Then he could see what had happened. The bullet had glanced on the ribs and furrowed under the flesh and jumped out again toward the back. If it had pierced through the ribs, it would have found the heart.

"Thank heaven," whispered Jingo. "I thought they had you. But you're going to live, Parson."

"Sure . . . I'm going to live . . . you fool," breathed the Parson.

He kept leaning against the rock, his head and shoulders both, but he put out his other arm and hung it loosely over Jingo and let the weight of that arm speak for him more than any words that he could have dug up out of his soul.

The little lines of reflection from the water kept running over that big, ugly face. They made the Parson seem about to speak. But still the only voice was the running of the stream.

Jingo looked out at it and saw how the current cut around the great stones that were scattered through the bed of the stream. He saw how the speed of the stream made the water lift a little as it leaped away from the rocks on the lower side, streaking out a wake. It was strange that the creek could run so fast and so smoothly—so smoothly that it kept throwing back the trembling reflection of the moonlight. But for all its speed, he saw the one thing that they could do.

"Parson," he said, "you can break the chain that holds my feet together . . . or my hands together? Can you do that? Smash the links between a couple of big rocks?"

The Parson had his eyes closed. He did not open them again, but he reached out and fumbled the ankle chains with his fingers. Then he shook his head in dissent.

Jingo looked down at the vast, moving head and understood. There was no hope of freedom for him. The key lay somewhere in the bottom of the creek. Not for the first time, he struggled to pull his hands through the grip of the manacles, and failed.

Then he heard footfalls coming back toward them among the rocks.

Chapter Twenty-Five

"They're going to hunt us down, and we got one gun between us . . . and three slugs in it," muttered the Parson. He kept his hand on his wounded side, and the blood steadily welled out between his fingers. But there was no use attempting to make a bandage to gird that vast barrel of a body—not until they had time to do the job thoroughly.

Jingo, staring down at the great, ugly face, wanted to find words so that he could speak what was in his heart, or a little of it. But then he knew that words were not necessary. They understood one another, and they would always understand.

"Parson," he said, "there's only one way out for us. They'll search till they find us. But if you can get across the stream and go down the farther side, you'll be able to get help here from the Tyrrel place."

"Yeah, sure. A coupla hours from now I could get help here from the Tyrrel place."

They had to whisper. The sound of footfalls no longer approached them. But they whispered at the ear of one another.

"And you'd be dead a long time before that," said the Parson.

"There's no other way," Jingo said. "You've got

to take your chance, and I'll stay here and take mine."

He nodded toward the stream.

"Plenty of rocks out there in the center. Once you get on the farther side of them, you'll be all right, Parson. You'll be fixed, all right. The boulders will shelter you from gunfire. The trip out to the center of the creek ought to be the only dangerous part of the business."

"All right," said the Parson. "Here goes."

He stood up and raised the revolver.

"Take the gun," said Jingo. "It's no good to me now. I could only absolutely . . ."

"You'd want me to walk off and leave you, would you?" said the Parson. He added sternly: "Take hold of that gun."

Jingo meekly grasped the rough handle of the Colt.

Then he was raised suddenly and thrown over the wide shoulder of the Parson. He tried to protest, but already the Parson was striding into the stream. The water deepened. It reached the feet of Jingo. It soaked him to the knees. Water rose to the very chin of the Parson, and Jingo felt the strong pulling of the current. If he felt it at all, how was the Parson able, in any way, to keep his footing?

Jingo scanned the shore they had left. As they advanced, it seemed that the boulders grew greater. He stared at the gaps between them, but there was no sight of the manhunters.

Aye, but there they were, suddenly—Wheeler Bent standing on top of a low rock, looking slowly up and down the ravine. Then there was Jake Rankin beside him. The moon glimmered on their guns.

Jingo looked behind him, over the shaggy head of the Parson. They were not many steps from the central rocks of the stream, but to a man carrying a heavy burden, and immersed to the chin in a strong current, every yard is a dangerous distance.

He was about to tell the Parson to hurry if he could—when the gunfire started.

A sightless something knifed through the water at the side of the Parson. Instantly came the report, flinging off the face of the stream and slapping against the ear of Jingo.

The Parson reached out his long arm, leaned as he strode forward, grasped the lower edge of the nearest rock, and swept himself and Jingo to the shelter behind it.

A bullet, at the same time, stung the ear of Jingo like a wasp. It had clipped away a bit of the lobe.

Then he found himself with the Parson behind the comfortable bulwark of the rock, safe.

But not really safe. There was only a narrow distance between them and the opposite shore, but that distance, small as it was, was totally impassable. Here the current had been compacted in a narrower throat, and the surface of the stream was streaked with little telltale bubbles of speed.

The force of the creek pulled at the legs of Jingo and carried them out aslant.

The weight of the irons on his ankles became a trifling thing compared with the sweep of the water.

All that Rankin and Wheeler Bent needed to do was to wait on the opposite shore until the two were finally torn from their grip on the rock.

The Parson, shuddering as the cold of the water entered his wound, said simply: "All right, Jingo. I guess we're gone. See if you can send the last three shots out of that there gun. Then we might as well take what's coming to us."

"That would only show that we're stuck here," said Jingo. "Otherwise . . . well, they won't know what's happening. They can't see what this water is like any more than we could when we were over there. They think that we're crawling ashore by this time."

"Aye, and what'll be done then?"

"Maybe they'll give up. Then, when they leave, we can go back across the creek the way we came."

"Maybe they'll come over after us," suggested the Parson.

"Maybe," agreed Jingo. He added: "Push me up a little, Parson. I'll take a look as carefully as I can and hope that they won't see me."

He was being lifted in the great hands of the Parson when the catastrophe came on them suddenly. Right over the brim of the big rock appeared the dripping body of Jake Rankin, with Wheeler Bent at his side.

Their guns were slung around their necks. They had only their hands to use against the Colt of Jingo, but the hand of Jake Rankin was as swift as the head of a striking snake. He caught Jingo's gun. One futile bullet rose at the face of the moon. Then Jingo, torn from the grasp of the astonished Parson, whirled down the current with Jake Rankin gripping him close.

The gun was the prize that Rankin wanted. And he had two hands to use. He kept his grip on the weapon with one hand. With the other he tried to beat Jingo to senselessness. And all the while the current swept them over and over. There was only a random chance now and then for Jingo to gulp in a breath of air. They swung around and around slowly. The force of the stream threw them to the side in a freakish eddy toward the shore from which they had come. Suddenly they were standing breast to breast, shoulder-high in the stream.

Well above them, Jingo saw the Parson standing up on the rock that had given them a moment of shelter. He saw Wheeler Bent entangled in the terrible arms of the giant. He heard the wild screech out of Bent's throat, and saw the limp body of the man flung down into the creek. Then the Parson plunged in and came toward his friend.

Jingo saw that as he ducked under the water to avoid a stranglehold that Rankin was trying to fasten on him.

Still his grasp was on the gun. They were staggering in toward the shore, through rapidly shoaling water, as Jingo received a heavy blow on the side of the head.

His wits spun. The clubbed hand of Rankin fell on him again. They were only knee-deep, with the shore beside them. Out of the distance, the tremendous lion's roar of the Parson gave promise of instant aid. Another voice, on a thinner and a higher note, was crying to him from the shore.

Through the whirl of his mind, moonlight and darkness and many images thronging across his eyes, he saw the girl coming toward him, running. She was in the water now, stretching out her hands, when another blow took the last strength out of the hands of Jingo. He had his wits and his eyes about him still. But he was loose as a wet rag, and out of his numbed fingers Rankin tore the revolver easily.

Jingo saw the gleam of it. It would be the last sight that came to him in this world, he was sure.

Something then came in between him and the sheen of the dripping Colt. That was the girl, flinging her arms back around his body, and with her head strained back as she strove to cover him from Rankin, who she faced.

He saw the big hand of Rankin go out to tear her

away from his quarry. He heard her crying out like a frightened animal.

The sound seemed to go through Rankin like a knife. His hand fell. He tried once more, and the scream stopped him.

"When you've got two hands to use," shouted Rankin suddenly, "I'll come back and get you, but only when there's nothing between us! Jingo, we ain't at the end of the road!"

He was out of the water and on the shore. He turned once at the side of a boulder and shook his fist at the pair who stood wavering in the stream. Then the great bulk of the Parson swept up on Jingo and the girl and bore them ashore.

Chapter Twenty-Six

They got pack mules from the ranch. That was the way the wounded were taken back to the Tyrrel place. Boyd, with his smashed face, was gone. Jake Rankin was gone, too, and they took the horses with them. Only Lizzie was left, for the good reason that even Rankin understood that she was useless except to her master.

It was on the back of Lizzie that the Parson placed Jingo, irons and all. He walked beside the big mare, leading her. A strange picture he made with the huge bandage that had been twisted around his body. But he kept laughing, in spite of the pain.

Wheeler Bent had been picked out of the edge of the stream, living indeed, but with a dozen bones broken in his body. He was packed on one mule, and Oliver, hovering between life and death, went up on another. The judge was there in person to supervise everything. The girl was there, too, being quick and efficient with her hands in the dressing of wounds, saying little, but now and again hunting out Jingo with her eyes.

That was how the procession went back to the ranch house finally, with Jingo in irons, but leading the way with the Parson.

When they got to the ranch, Farrell came with

some files out of the blacksmith shop and began to cut the manacles from Jingo's hands and feet. The files screeched on terrible, grinding notes, but no one seemed to mind the noise. No one minded anything, except that tragedy had come and gone again.

There were a good many things to remember.

The torn flesh of the forearms of the Parson was one picture that would not be forgotten. When they were bandaged, he refused to go to bed. A big Indian blanket was huddled around his torso, and he sat up and drank whiskey out of a big tumbler. Every breath he drew must have tormented his flesh, but he would not notice pain.

He kept shouting out: "Here's to Jingo . . . long may he jingle, and never jangle! Here's to you, Jingo, old son!"

The girl sat close to the Parson, and kept looking him in the face, nodding and smiling as though every moment she were discovering more matter for wonder.

But he had not so much as a glance for her. When the irons at last were filed off the hands and ankles of Jingo, the Parson scooped them up off the floor and hurled them to the roof, high up among the shadowy beams. They fell again with a crash, but even Judge Tyrrel appreciated this jest.

Afterward the cook came in with word that Wheeler Bent was asking for Jingo.

"For me?" Jingo said. "No . . . he may be asking for the devil, for he'd never ask for me."

"It's you that he wants to see," the cook insisted.

So Jingo, after one almost frightened glance around the room, went off to the chamber where Bent was lying. They had put his legs and arms in splints. He was swathed in bandages. One side of his face was frightfully swollen and discolored where a fist of the Parson had glanced from the flesh. The effect of the blow had been sufficient to close one eye completely, and even the bright little golden mustache seemed dim and was twisted awry. The other eye held steadily on Jingo.

"Thanks for coming," he said. "I've got a few words to say to you, Jingo."

Jingo tried to find some honest word in his heart. None was there, and he could only hold silence.

"I wanted to say," Wheeler Bent began, "that I'm glad it turned out this way. I don't care how long the prison term may be. I'm going to be glad that it turned out this way. It's better . . . it's a sight better to be in jail than to be a murderer and free to walk about."

Jingo came suddenly closer and looked down into the battered face.

"By the leaping old thunder," Jingo said, "sometimes it takes a lot of hammering to make the steel right."

He held out his hand.

The one eye of Wheeler Bent widened.

"Do you mean it?" he asked. "Don't do it unless you mean it."

"I mean it," Jingo assured him. And he shook hands with Wheeler Bent.

"Will you tell Gene?" asked Wheeler Bent.

"I'll tell her everything," Jingo said.

"Then," said Wheeler Bent, "I'm halfway out of hell already."

It was not many days after this that the Parson lay aslant in the longest and widest double bed in the house of Judge Tyrrel. Lying in this fashion, he was barely able to give himself sufficient room to lie straight. There was gloom in the heart of the Parson, but since a slight fever persisted, the doctor had insisted that he remain in bed for another day or two.

Judge Tyrrel, seated near the window, was helping the Parson to kill time.

"And as for you, Parson?" said the judge finally. "What is there that I can do for you?"

The Parson considered for a long time. At last he shook his head and answered.

"I gotta wear my own clothes. I can't put on the other gent's coat, or his ideas, neither. And I can't shorten up my step, neither, to the walk other gents walk. There'd be only one thing you could do for me, and that would be to turn Jingo loose to go on the trail with me again. Well, I reckon you can't do that. I reckon that nobody is ever going to be able to turn Jingo loose again."

Out of the distance just then came a sudden chorus of laughter from a woman's voice and a man's.

"No, I guess nobody ever will be able to do that," said the judge.

About the Author

Max Brand is the best-known pen name of Frederick Faust, creator of Dr. Kildare, Destry, and many other fictional characters popular with readers and viewers worldwide. Faust wrote for a variety of audiences in many genres. His enormous output, totaling approximately thirty million words or the equivalent of five hundred thirty ordinary books, covered nearly every field: crime, fantasy, historical romance, espionage, Westerns, science fiction, adventure, animal stories, love, war, and fashionable society, big business and big medicine. Eighty motion pictures have been based on his work along with many radio and television programs. For good measure he also published four volumes of poetry. Perhaps no other author has reached more people in more different ways.

Born in Seattle in 1892, orphaned early, Faust grew up in the rural San Joaquin Valley of California. At Berkeley he became a student rebel and one-man literary movement, contributing prodigiously to all campus publications. Denied a degree because of unconventional conduct, he embarked on a series of adventures culminating in New York City where, after a period of near starvation, he received simultaneous recognition as a serious poet and successful author of fiction. Later, he traveled widely, making his home in New York, then in Florence, Italy, and finally in Los Angeles.

Once the United States entered the Second World War, Faust abandoned his lucrative writing career and his work as a screenwriter to serve as a war correspondent with the infantry in Italy, despite his fifty-one years and a bad heart. He was killed during a night attack on a hilltop village held by the German army. New books based on magazine serials or unpublished manuscripts or restored versions continue to appear so that, alive or dead, he has averaged a new book every four months for seventy-five years. Beyond this, some work by him is newly reprinted every week of every year in one or another format somewhere in the world. A great deal more about this author and his work can be found in *The Max Brand Companion* (Greenwood Press, 1997) edited by Jon Tuska and Vicki Piekarski. His Website is www.MaxBrandOnline.com.

Center Point Large Print
600 Brooks Road / PO Box 1
Thorndike, ME 04986-0001 USA

(207) 568-3717

US & Canada:
1 800 929-9108
www.centerpointlargeprint.com